RAGWEED

Avon Camelot Books by
Avi

AMANDA JOINS THE CIRCUS
KEEP YOUR EYE ON AMANDA!

THE BARN
BEYOND THE WESTERN SEA, BOOK I: THE ESCAPE FROM HOME
BEYOND THE WESTERN SEA, BOOK II: LORD KIRKLE'S MONEY
BLUE HERON
THE MAN WHO WAS POE
PUNCH WITH JUDY
ROMEO AND JULIET—TOGETHER (AND ALIVE!) AT LAST
SOMETHING UPSTAIRS
S.O.R. LOSERS
TOM, BABETTE & SIMON
THE TRUE CONFESSIONS OF CHARLOTTE DOYLE
"WHO WAS THAT MASKED MAN, ANYWAY?"
WINDCATCHER

TALES FROM DIMWOOD FOREST:
POPPY
POPPY AND RYE
RAGWEED

Avon Flare Books

NOTHING BUT THE TRUTH
A PLACE CALLED UGLY
SOMETIMES I THINK I HEAR MY NAME

**To find out more about Avi, visit his website at
www.avi-writer.com**

RAGWEED

by AVI

illustrated by Brian Floca

AN AVON  CAMELOT BOOK

AVON BOOKS, INC.
1350 Avenue of the Americas
New York, New York 10019

Text copyright © 1999 by Avi
Illustrations copyright © 1999 by Brian Floca
Illustrations by Brian Floca
The illustrations are drawn with Eberhard Faber Design Ebony pencils on
Stonehenge paper.
Interior design by Kellan Peck
ISBN: 0-380-97690-0

Library of Congress Cataloging in Publication Data:

Avi, 1937–
Ragweed / Avi; illustrated by Brian Floca.
p.   cm. — (An Avon Camelot book)
Prequel to: Poppy.
Summary: Ragweed, a young country mouse, leaves his family and
travels to the big city, where he finds excitement and danger
and sees cats for the first time.
[1. Mice—Fiction. 2. Cats—Fiction.] I. Floca, Brian, ill.
II. Title.   98-55160
PZ7.A953Rag   1999   CIP
[Fic]—dc21   AC

First Avon Camelot Printing: May 1999

CAMELOT TRADEMARK REG. U.S. PAT. OFF. AND IN OTHER COUNTRIES, MARCA REGISTRADA,
HECHO EN U.S.A.

Printed in the U.S.A.

OPM   10 9 8 7 6 5 4 3 2

www.avonbooks.com

FOR SUZI LEE

Contents

Map: *Amperville*   x–xi
1. Ragweed   1
2. Some Advice Is Given   7
3. Silversides   13
4. To the City   21
5. Clutch   29
6. F.E.A.R.   35
7. Blinker   40
8. The Cheese Squeeze Club   46
9. What Happened at the Cheese Squeeze Club   58
10. Blinker, Continued   63
11. Windshield and Foglight   68
12. Silversides   78
13. Ragweed Wanders   84
14. Ragweed Makes Up His Mind   92
15. Trapped in the Garbage Pile   100
16. Some Ideas   109
17. Silversides   114
18. Ragweed's Plan   118

19. A Coming Together   126
20. The Great Cleanup   131
21. Silversides Learns Some Things   138
22. Blinker Makes a Report   143
23. Opening Night at Café Independent   150
24. The Sewer   159
25. The Show at Café Independent   165
26. In the Basement   170
27. A Goodbye   175

RAGWEED

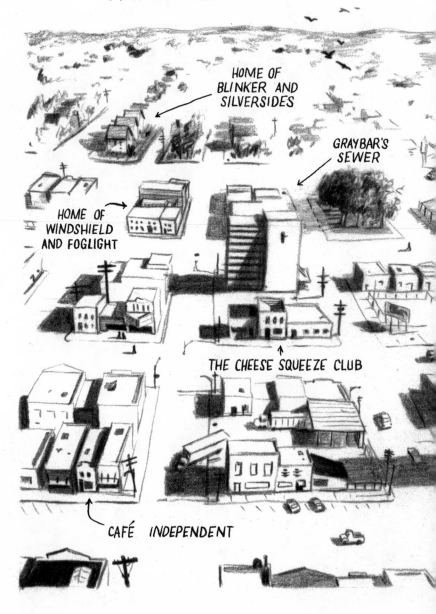

AMPERVILLE

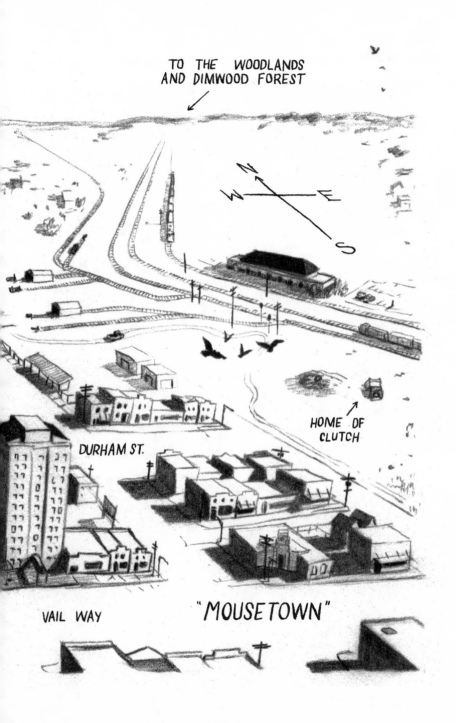

1
Ragweed

"Ma, a mouse has to do what a mouse has to do."

Ragweed, a golden mouse with dark orange fur, round ears and a not very long tail, was saying goodbye to his mother and father as well as to fifty of his brothers and sisters. They were all gathered by the family nest, which was situated just above the banks of the Brook.

"Is it . . . something about *us* that's making you leave home?" his mother, whose name was Clover, asked tearfully. She was small and round, with silky black eyes.

"Aw, Ma, that's not fair," Ragweed replied, wishing he could leave without so much fuss. "I just want to see things. I *am* almost four months old, you know. I mean, the Brook *is* wonderful, but . . . well, it's not the whole world."

Ragweed's father, Valerian, drew himself up. He was long-faced and lanky, and his scruffy whiskers were touched with gray. "Now, son," he said, "no need to poke fun at us stay-at-homes."

"I'm sorry, Dad. I didn't mean to joke. All I'm doing is going off to explore what else there is. You know, before settling down. I won't be gone long."

"Will you absolutely promise to come back?" Clover asked. Though Ragweed had carefully slicked down his fur so that it was quite neat and proper, she found a small strand around his ear that required careful adjusting. But then, Ragweed was very special to her.

"Of course I will," Ragweed assured her, trying to duck his mother's fussy fixing.

"And . . . and . . . if you meet a young female mouse," Clover added gently, "one for whom you develop a . . . a fondness, just make sure she . . . she really cares for you."

Ragweed blushed. "Hey, Ma, I'm too young for that stuff. Anyway, if I'm going to get someplace today, I better start moving."

This notice of his imminent departure caused Clover to fling her paws around Ragweed's neck and give him a nuzzle about his right ear. "Please, *please* be cautious!" she whispered. "Promise me that you will."

"I promise," Ragweed returned.

A reluctant Clover released her son.

Valerian held out his paw. "Ragweed," he said, "you're a clear-thinking, straight-talking, hard-working young mouse. I'm proud of you."

Ragweed shook his father's paw. "Dad," he replied, "if I can be anything like you, that'll be good enough for me."

"Thank you, son," Valerian said, his voice husky.

Embarrassed by so much emotion, Ragweed looked sheepishly at his brothers and sisters. Of those still at home, he was the eldest. Even among the older ones— who had returned from nearby homes to say goodbye— Ragweed was the first to leave the area of the Brook. Hardly a wonder that they were gazing at him with affectionate awe. But it was to Rye, his younger brother by a few weeks, that Ragweed went.

Rye looked very much like Ragweed, save for a notch in his right ear, the result of an accident.

"Okay, Rye," Ragweed said, giving his brother a mock punch on the shoulder. "You're the big kid in the nest now. Make sure you take care of things. If you don't, hey, you're going to answer to me when I come back. Get it?"

"I know," Rye replied with a grin masking his annoyance that his older brother was telling him what to do.

Next, Ragweed tipped a wink to his favorite younger sister, Thistle. "See you around, kiddo," he called.

"Oh, Ragweed, I'm going to miss you *so* much!" she cried. Rushing forward, she gave Ragweed a big nuzzle.

Ragweed, determined to be lighthearted, stepped back, gave a carefree wave, and set off up the hill, striding boldly toward the ridge that overlooked the little valley. Halfway up he came to a large boulder embedded in an outcropping of earth. There he paused and looked down at his family, who were still observing his departure. Though he wanted to move on, Ragweed found himself lingering.

The spring air was brimming with a delicate sweetness; the vaulting blue sky seemed endless, the sun warm and embracing. Amid moss and grass, flowers had burst forth with youthful daring, in contrast to the shallow old Brook, which wound lazily between low, leafy banks, bearing pink and white water lilies on its wide surface. As for the tall trees that stood all around, they were veiled in a downy green mist of just-born leaves.

What lay below Ragweed was not merely beautiful, it was home. *His* home. And there was his family, whom he loved as much as he knew they loved him.

Hope I'm doing what's right, he thought with a sigh. Then, reminding himself out loud that "A mouse has to do what a mouse has to do," he gave a final wave to his family and continued up the ridge.

Ragweed had no notion where he was heading. He had consulted no one, planned little. "I'll just go where whim takes me," he'd told Rye.

As Ragweed went along he now and again broke into snatches of an old song. His voice was good—if rather low for a mouse—and he enjoyed singing. The song he trilled was one he and his family often sang on hikes and picnics.

"A mouse will a-roving go,
  Along wooded paths and pebbled ways
  To places high and places low,
  Where birds do sing 'neath sunny rays,
  For the world is full of mice, oh!
  For the world is full of mice, oh!"

The song carried him to the crest of yet another hill. There he paused again. The trail seemed to extend from his toes straight out to the horizon. Just to see it gave him the wonderful sensation that anything might happen. He took a deep breath. How delicious was the sense of freedom he felt. How fine that he and he alone was responsible for himself. He had not—he now realized—grasped how exciting it would be to grow up and strike out on one's own.

The thought of it all brought a tingling from the tip of his nose to the tip of his tail.

Energized anew, Ragweed stepped boldly along the trail, now and again squeaking out at top voice, "For the world is full of mice, oh!"

2

Some Advice Is Given

All that morning Ragweed continued until he reached a split in the pathway. One path went due east. The other headed south. For the first time since he'd left home he had to make a decision as to which direction to go.

Relishing the luxury of making up his mind at leisure, he decided to rest. Then, remembering that he had not eaten that day, he nosed about until he found enough hazelnuts to make himself a lunch. Hazelnuts were Ragweed's favorite food.

As Ragweed nibbled away, an elderly vole meandered out from behind a bush. The vole had a short tail, large ears, reddish-brown fur on his back, and gray whiskers on his blunt snout. He was also nearsighted, snuffling so intently about the ground that he walked right into Ragweed.

"Oh, my, oh, my," the vole exclaimed, flustered and embarrassed. "I do beg a thousand pardons. I didn't see you, young fellow. Really! What's come over me? Walking

into strangers. I fear my eyes are not what they used to be. Do forgive me."

"No harm done, sir," Ragweed returned cheerfully. "I'm sprawled where I probably shouldn't be, an idle wanderer from the Brook. I suppose you've heard of it."

"I'm afraid I haven't," the vole said apologetically.

Ragweed, thrilled by the thought that he had already come far enough to be a stranger, said, "That's even better." Then he asked, "Are you from around here?"

"Indeed I am," the vole returned. "I've lived in these parts for more years than I'd like to admit. What brings you here, young fellow?"

"I'm off to see the world."

"Off to see the world, eh?" the vole echoed, yearning and regret mingling in his voice. "Well, it's a mighty big place, this world."

"Have you seen it?" Ragweed asked with keen interest.

"Just a tad," the vole said, making a humble gesture that managed to imply a very great deal more. "Of course, that was when I was younger. Oh, yes, the world is fascinating."

Ragweed considered the vole with new eyes. Clearly, here was a creature of vast experience. "Sir," the mouse inquired, "might you know, then, where these two paths lead?"

"I should hope I would," the vole returned with a touch of pride. "In my time, young fellow, I've traveled both. They'll take you to completely opposite places. This one goes east to a forest. Dimwood Forest, to be precise. A most impressive place. Dark. Strange. Beautiful. Something you should experience. Just watch out for owls," he added.

"I'm sure I'd like it," Ragweed said, paying no heed to the warning. "What about the other?"

"The one to the south? It goes to a railway."

Ragweed blinked. "What's a . . . railway?"

"Forgive me," the vole said. "I didn't mean to presume. A railway is made by humans. You do know about humans?"

"Oh, yes," Ragweed replied, though he had not in fact actually seen one.

"Well, now, humans make trains. A train sits on a track. That's to say, two rails allowing it to go places. The whole apparatus is absolutely gigantic. Makes an astonishing noise. Goes at staggering speeds. But if I add that they're dangerous, I'm putting it mildly."

"You said humans use these trains for going places," Ragweed said, fascinated. "What kind of places?"

"Towns. Cities."

"I'm afraid I don't know what they are either," Ragweed confessed.

"Oh, my, my—we are young, aren't we?" the vole said.

Blushing, Ragweed said, "I'm only four months old."

"You'll get over that soon enough!" The vole chuckled at his own little joke. "Well now, my young fellow, a town or a city is where great numbers of humans live. As you know, humans build the most amazing nests. Prodigious constructions. Reach the sky, they do. As for a town or a city . . . Well, look at those trees over there. Now use your imagination. Instead of a tree, picture a human's nest. Multiply that one nest by a thousand, two thousand! No! Twenty thousand! A million! There! You have a city."

"Oh, wow!" Ragweed cried. "But does anything happen there?"

"*Does anything happen!*" the vole echoed, paw over his heart. "Young fellow, if you had a year to spare I might begin to tell you stories about cities that would curl your tail. Why, *everything* happens in cities. Mind, it can be hazardous for creatures like you and me."

"But . . . exciting?"

"*Exciting?*" the vole said with a whisper and a wink. "That's where they invented the word."

"That sounds like the perfect place for me," Ragweed said, jumping up. "Thanks for your advice."

"I'm not aware I was giving any advice," the vole said wistfully. "Actually, I think you should go to Dimwood Forest first."

"Why?"

"It's safer."

"Next time!" Ragweed shouted, already hurrying down the path that led to the railway.

"Oh, dear," the vole said as he watched Ragweed scamper away. He had recollected something of great importance he should have told Ragweed. "Young fellow!" he cried out. "If you reach a city, keep on the lookout for cats! Cities are full of them!"

Ragweed, however, was gone. The warning went unheard.

All that afternoon Ragweed hurried along the trail, reaching a deep gully just at dusk. Peering into it he saw something he had never seen before—a railway train. At first Ragweed could do nothing but stare at it, so astonishing was its size. Not only was it amazingly tall, he found it impossible to see either end.

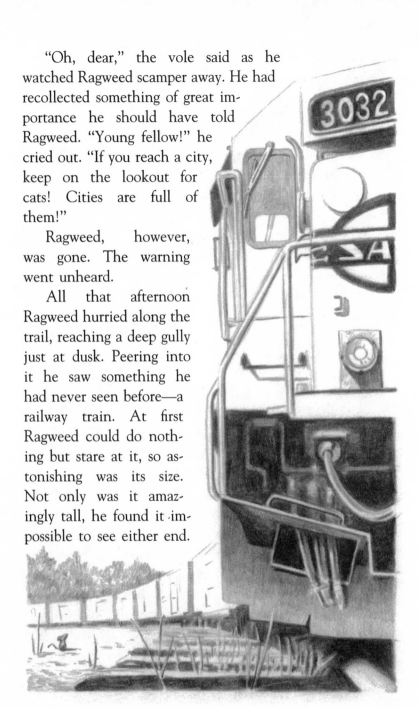

He did see wheels—enormous, shiny steel ones—but they were not turning. Yet Ragweed was quite certain the old vole had said the train *went* to cities, though he could not begin to imagine how it managed the trip.

The part of the train that sat before Ragweed was a boxcar. "Great Western Trail" was written large on its dull red sides of corrugated steel. The name charmed Ragweed, speaking to him of great adventures. Even better, the door was open.

Full of the desire to explore, Ragweed scurried into the gully. Approaching the tracks, he found a low coupling hose hanging between two boxcars. He leaped on the coupling, climbed up it, then ran along a rain gutter on the side of the car. Within moments he was inside.

The boxcar appeared to be empty. Then Ragweed spied a split sack labeled "Oats" in a corner. Though he did not exactly know what oats were, he knew good food when he smelled it. Besides, he was hungry. The day had been exciting but long.

"This is the life," he murmured as he pushed his nose into the oats and began to munch. He was still gorging himself when the train gave a sudden lurch.

"Hey! What's happening?" Ragweed cried and rushed to the open door. To his amazement the boxcar was moving. At first it did not go very fast. Within moments, however, it was rattling along at speeds far greater than Ragweed ever could have imagined.

With a sense of shock Ragweed realized that his woodland home was very quickly fading away. His heart experienced a painful squeeze. Not only was he now truly going to see the world, there was no turning back.

The young mouse, in a voice that managed to combine joy and sorrow, cried, "City, here I come!"

3
Silversides

ilversides was not just another white cat. She was a very angry cat. According to her, the world had become a terrible place, and the cause of it all was mice.

A large cat, Silversides was seven years old, in the very prime of life. Her eyes were yellow, her fur white as snow. Around her neck was a pink polyvinyl collar studded with sparkling diamond-like sequins. Dangling from this collar was her city license—"Amperville 30"—a tag she wore with pride. Low numbers were prized among Amperville's many cats.

Silversides lived in the home into which she had been carried as an eight-week-old kitten. Most recently her private place was a rug behind a growling basement furnace. The house humans came by this warm, quiet spot only rarely, which meant that these days Silversides was alone most of the time. This did not please her.

Though Silversides had raised twelve kittens during her mothering years, she had done it by herself. It had not been easy tending her litters. It required continual struggle to teach the kittens to grow into decent hardworking, right-thinking cats. As far as she was concerned, she had succeeded. Now they were grown and gone, having chosen homes of their own. There were even grand-kittens.

Though Silversides saw these youngsters only occasionally—on midnight strolls, while she was patrolling her territory or hunting in the park—she fretted about them all the time. Life in the city of Amperville was not what it once had been.

When Silversides had been young, Amperville had been prosperous, clean, and wholesome. Mice were relatively few. Now—she had no idea why—the humans who bore the prime responsibility for keeping things up no longer cared much about Amperville. The community was run-down. The worst result was that the city had become infested by mice. Moreover, these mice were very different from those of previous generations.

In the good old days—according to Silversides—house mice knew their place and numbers. Timid and respectful,

these mice lived, with gratitude, on crumbs. They entered houses furtively, and then only through back doors or cracks in foundations.

Only rarely did these mice make themselves noticeable. To do otherwise was to put their lives at risk, as both cats and mice understood.

When the occasional rebellious house mouse got uppity, Amperville cats knew exactly what to do with them. The upstart mouse would be caught and . . . dealt with. No fuss. No muss. Nothing needed to be said.

But nowadays Amperville mice had not just increased in number, they had become brazen. They acted as if they actually had a right to be in Amperville, going so far as to claim part of town—a section by the railroad that humans had abandoned—as their own. Mouse

Town, they called it. They had their own mayor, schools, clubs.

Though Silversides tried at first to ignore these new mice, every one of them was a personal insult, an unending irritation, a reminder that things were not as they should be.

Then two things of great importance happened.

The girl who lived in Silversides's house brought home a white-furred, pink-eyed mouse and kept it in her room. She called this mouse Blinker. The mouse's very name—sickeningly cute—irritated Silversides enormously. That she and this mouse were the same color only served to inflame the cat even more.

There had been a time when Silversides had slept on the girl's pillow. If she wasn't sleeping on the pillow, she was on the rug at the foot of the girl's bed. Now the girl lavished all her affection on the mouse. She fondled him, kissed him, carried him around, gave Blinker the complete freedom of her room. Worst of all, the girl told Silversides that she was no longer welcome there. The rug had been removed to the basement.

Insulted and humiliated, Silversides hid behind the furnace for days on end. There she brooded and sulked, deeply depressed, preferring the darkness of the cellar and the smelly litter box to any kind of social life, indoors or out.

Only now and again did Silversides venture forth. When she did, it was to visit her grown-up kittens and grand-kittens. It was just such a visit that brought about a second crisis, one that changed the course of Silversides's life.

Jasper was a particular favorite grand-kitten of Silversides's. He was an affectionate coal-black creature with blue eyes and a splash of white upon his chest.

One day Silversides came to visit Jasper only to discover him playing on the front lawn with a . . . mouse. Silversides's first reaction was astonishment. The next moment she was filled with rage.

Leaping forward, she gave the mouse a few hard smacks, which sent him reeling away. Then she cuffed her grand-kitten smartly across the nose.

"How dare you!" she howled.

Jasper, frightened as well as upset by Silversides's actions, hardly knew what to say. "That was my best friend," he mewed piteously.

"Friend!" Silversides screeched. "You ought to be ashamed of yourself. Aren't there any decent cats in this neighborhood for you to play with? Don't you know that the lowliest cat is vastly superior to the highest mouse? Where's your mother? I intend to give her a piece of my paw!"

A cowering Jasper said, "My mother went out."

"Where?"

"I don't know. Business."

"Business!" Silversides screeched. "A mother's business is to stay home and make sure her children have proper friends! I cannot believe how far this town has fallen!"

With that she stalked away, tail erect, but not before she had given her grand-kitten a spank on his bottom.

This incident changed Silversides's life. Her anger was so great she made up her mind to do something about the Amperville mouse problem.

That night she began to prowl the streets of the city in search of mice. It was not the act of a hungry cat seeking food. It was vengeance.

Sure enough, Silversides came upon two mice. The

first was sent running for its life. The second did not run fast enough and met a grisly end. Silversides deposited the corpse outside the girl's door. It was meant to be a declaration of war.

Silversides quickly realized she could not solve the city's mouse problem all on her own. She created an organization. The organization was dedicated to keeping cats on top, people in the middle, mice on the bottom. Silversides called her group Felines Enraged About Rodents, or "F.E.A.R." She even created a slogan for F.E.A.R.: "Felines First."

Though Silversides invited other cats to join F.E.A.R., most could not be bothered. They would shrug or say things like "I don't need to join a club to catch mice. I do just fine on my own." Or "I like having more mice around. There's that many more to chase." And even "Rude, food, they taste the same."

In the end, from the entire cat population of Amperville, Silversides was able to recruit only one other cat for her organization. The two formed the membership of Felines Enraged About Rodents. Silversides was president. Her vice president was a cat by the name of Graybar.

Graybar was a street cat. Scruffy gray in color, he was lean and covered with scars to prove his meanness. He had a jagged ear and a limp, the result of a battle about which he was particularly proud. It had been three against one, and he had been the one. And he had been the winner. He bore his injuries as proof of his toughness.

"Do you want to know what I think of mice?" Graybar asked Silversides when she first talked to him about joining F.E.A.R.

"Yes."

"The only good mouse is a dead mouse."

"You're my kind of cat," Silversides said.

Silversides had learned that country mice often came to town by train. These trains stopped near Mouse Town and mice got off. One of the first things Silversides and Graybar did was organize a patrol around the old railway depot. Mice new to town, timid and often scared, were easy prey for the organization.

When Silversides or Graybar caught such a mouse, they terrified it, warned it never to return, then threw it back onto the train. These were the lucky ones.

4
To the City

All that night the freight train carrying Ragweed rumbled on. He was too excited to sleep. Instead, he remained by the open door and watched the passing scene. And pass it did. One rapid vision after another flashed before his eager eyes. No sooner did he see something of great interest—barely grasping what it was—than it vanished, to be replaced by something just as new, just as fascinating. The one constant was the moon, which remained in the night sky like an old friend.

At first there were many trees, but there were fewer as the train rushed on. There were also structures, large and dark, which fit the description the old vole had provided for human nests. Now and again they contained gleaming lights. Once the mouse thought he saw the silhouetted form of a human pacing before what looked like a window. It went by so quickly, however, that it was impossible to be sure.

Sometimes there were clusters of these human nests.

Ragweed—again recalling the vole's words—decided these clusters were towns.

It made him wonder where the train was heading. Not that there was any question about getting off while it was moving. That would have been foolish. But when the train stopped, should he jump off right away or wait for some other place?

Laughing at himself, Ragweed acknowledged the wonderful fact that it did not matter where he got off: Everything he saw and did would be new. It was just the life he desired. So he sat and watched and thirsted for more.

The train, clacking rhythmically over the rails, rushed on through the night. Now and again its whistle blew. Long, low, and melodic it was, the most powerful sound that Ragweed had ever heard. He decided it was the train's song: the song of a wanderer, a song about a heroic search for adventures far from home. Humming along, he made it his own.

It was not until dawn that the train began to slow down. Ragweed had fallen asleep at last, but the moment

the train reduced its speed he woke, alert and watching intently.

There were many human nests to see now. All in neat rows they were, with prim grassy areas before them, as well as an occasional tree. How orderly, Ragweed thought with puzzlement. He decided he must be coming to a city. Sure enough, within moments he spied a large sign. It read:

WELCOME TO AMPERVILLE!
A CLEAN, DECENT PLACE TO LIVE AND WORK

For the first time he saw humans clearly. He was shocked by their size, by how little fur they had, how each one was covered by a different mix of colors. He also spotted what looked like little trains. They were boxlike metallic things, brightly colored, each with a human inside and two bright lights in front. There were many of them and they moved very fast.

Heart beating fast with anticipation, Ragweed edged

closer to the doorway, stuck his nose over the threshold, and peered down. It was a long way. Nonetheless he prepared himself to leap.

But the train did not stop. It continued to roll with just enough speed to make a premature departure dangerous.

Other human nests passed by. Soon, however, they grew fewer in number. And those that Ragweed saw seemed run-down, wrecked. Here and there, he saw more of those metallic boxes. They were not moving. Instead, they appeared to have been discarded, torn apart. One or two were even upside down, with wheels to the sky like a dead creature, their bright colors turned to a uniform dark brown.

The train slowed to a crawl. A series of bumps and thumps followed until it came to a complete halt. The whistle sounded a long, low mournful shriek, as if to say goodbye.

Not far from the train Ragweed spied a number of dilapidated human nests. They looked abandoned. Among scrawny bushes there were more of those broken, twisted metallic boxes.

Closer by was a heap of objects containing food bits, bottles, cans, boxes, paper—the sorts of things that sometimes mysteriously found their way to the Brook—plus lots of other things Ragweed could not identify. Nearby was another pile, this one made of what looked like chunks of white clay. The whole scene appeared grim and lifeless.

Then he glanced down at the ground right beneath him. Sitting amid the gravel, long fluffy tail waving menacingly, was a large, furry white beast.

In all his life Ragweed had never actually seen a cat. Like all mice, however, he knew a great deal about them by way of countless scary stories. So it was that Ragweed needed only to see Silversides to know that here was a cat, and she was his enemy.

Sure enough, the cat called out in a shrill, angry voice, "If I were you, mouse, I'd keep going. Amperville doesn't like strangers. Certainly not strangers who are mice. This is a clean, decent place." To make her point, she opened her mouth wide, revealing a pink tongue, a deep dark gullet, and many sharp white teeth.

Ragweed was too horrified to say or do anything.

Not so the cat. She hissed, then spat, spewing upon Ragweed. The next moment, though she had been sitting, she leaped into the boxcar. She would have landed right on Ragweed if the frightened mouse had not lost his footing and tumbled.

Landing on the gravel by the side of the train tracks, a frantic Ragweed twisted around and looked up. The white cat glared angrily down at him from the boxcar. "If you're looking for a fight, mouse, you've come to the right town!" she said. Tensing her muscles, she prepared to jump again.

Ragweed did not wait. He bolted up and began to run as fast as he could. A thud sounded behind. Without looking, he knew the cat was after him. "Outsider!" Silversides screeched. "Stranger!"

Searching desperately for a place of safety, Ragweed dashed on. He stole a glance over his shoulder. The cat was loping along behind him, a horrid grin upon her face. She was enjoying the chase. "Get out of town, mouse!" she screeched. "Felines First! F.E.A.R. rules! Leave on your own before you're dragged out by your tail!"

Desperate, Ragweed dove into the jumble of junk he'd observed from the boxcar and crawled into a can, only to find himself knee-deep in gooey red sauce. Almost faint from the fumes, he shot out of the can and became momentarily entangled in a twist of wires. Pulling free, he paused to listen. The cat was right behind him.

From the wires Ragweed squeezed under moldy pages full of words, worked his way around some collapsed boxes—the words "Corn Flakes" were on one of them— then crawled over old pickles and reeking tubs of decaying food. That brought him to the other side of the pile.

He looked out. Fifteen yards in front of him were some run-down human nests. But before them sat one of those large metallic boxes, of a rusty brown color. Not only did the box appear to be broken, but its wheels were hard to see, sunk deep into the earth. On the side of the one nearest Ragweed was a small hole at ground level. He was

sure that if he could get through that hole, he would be safe from the cat.

Crouching, he listened intently for some hint as to the cat's location. What he heard was more pushing and pulling suggesting the cat was still behind him, but getting closer. Ragweed was sure he had no choice. To stay meant certain death. He had to bolt. "Farewell, Mom," he whispered. "Farewell, Dad!"

With that he galloped out from beneath the pile. Almost instantly there was a hideous yowl behind him. Without looking Ragweed knew the cat was on his tail. This time she was not holding back.

The mouse ran as he'd never run in his life, great bounding, stiff-tailed leaps that took him closer and closer to the metal box. But when he reached it he discovered to his horror that the hole was blocked from the inside by a piece of wood.

Desperate, he clawed at the wood. It did not budge. He looked back. The cat was crouching, barely a yard away, belly low to the ground, yellow eyes fixed on him like daggers. Sequins flashing, claws flexed, tail waving, rump wiggling, the cat was preparing her deadly pounce.

5
Clutch

Ragweed pressed against the blocked hole—only to have it suddenly open. A paw reached out, grabbed Ragweed's shoulder, and pulled him forcibly inside. Then, just as Silversides was completing her pounce, the piece of wood—for that was what had been blocking the hole—slammed in her face.

Stunned, a panting Ragweed lay upon a not very clean rug. It took a moment before he could focus. A female mouse was looking down at him.

She was tall and thin as a stick, though her leanness suggested toughness, nothing brittle. Her fur was gray-brown in color, except for the top of her head, which had been dyed green. Her nose was blunt, her whiskers poorly groomed. From her left ear dangled a purple plastic bead at the end of a tiny chain.

"Hey, dude, what's up?" she said.

Ragweed blinked. "What?"

"Like, Silversides almost snuff you, mouse?"

"Silversides?"

"Hey, mouse, you saying you didn't see that sucker coming down on you?"

"You mean . . . that cat?"

The mouse laughed. "Like, she wasn't a bus, was she?"

Not understanding what was being said to him, Ragweed looked around the space into which he had been pulled. It had a lofty ceiling with windows all around the top. At one end there was a wheel attached to a bar that stuck out from a wall. Other stick-like things rose up from the floor.

"What is this . . . place?" Ragweed asked.

"It's a Ford Mustang," the mouse replied. "Sixty-six. Hardtop. Like, tight, right?"

"Oh," Ragweed said, not particularly enlightened.

The car was astonishingly messy. Off to one side was an unkempt mound of shredded cloth—a bed, Ragweed guessed. Crumbs lay scattered everywhere. Pieces of paper littered the area. A strip of wood with four wheels—Rag-weed had no idea what that was—had been tossed into a corner. A wooden spoon on which several strings had been stretched from the narrow end to the wide end was affixed to a wall.

"You got a name, dude?" the mouse asked.

"Ragweed."

"That's cool," the mouse said. "What's it mean?"

"Mean? Well, I suppose it's a plant. But I never think of it that way."

"Awesome," the city mouse said and held out a paw.

Ragweed offered his, but instead of shaking it, the house mouse slapped it. "Gotcha!" she said.

"May I ask your name?" Ragweed inquired politely.

"Clutch."

"Clutch?"

"Clutch, dude, like in a car."

"And . . . and a . . . car?" Ragweed inquired.

Clutch laughed. "What you're sitting in, dude. Big metal things, on wheels. With motors, stink, and noise. They haul people around."

"Oh, yes. And . . . thanks for saving me."

"Hey, no problem. See, that Silversides is an uptown cat. She and her pal, Graybar, hang around, you know, sort of like guards. Like, they go for any little meat on the feet with a different beat. Know what I'm saying? Bad to the bone."

Ragweed shuddered. "I guess."

"I mean, she heads up an organization called Felines Enraged About Rodents. F.E.A.R. Trying to keep the town clean and pure. Like, they don't want any riffraff—that's us mice—coming in. And what's already here, see, has to be right, decent, and respectful. That is, right, decent, and respectful according to *them*. Know what I'm saying?"

"What's a rodent?" Ragweed asked.

"Like, a fancy name for mouse," Clutch said. "Hey, mouse, exactly how new are you around here?"

"I . . . just got off the train."

"From the country?"

"How did you know?"

"Hey, I see it all the time. The train pulls in. Dudes getting off to take a peek. Know what I'm saying? Trying to get a life, right? Wanting to check things out. But, like, you're all so green the grass is envious."

"Oh," Ragweed said.

"Anyway, welcome to where it's at, mouse. You want action, you've planted right. Like, I'm saying, dude, this place—Mouse Town—ain't pretty, but, hey, it's cool. This town hops. This town does tricks. You do it right, it's totally rave. Awesome. Check it out."

Ragweed blinked. "I beg your pardon."

"Like, this is phat city," Clutch went on. "It's down. Sweet. Tight. Out of town, downtown. The hot spot. It rules. You cool enough to hang with me, dude?"

"Actually, I'm quite warm," replied an utterly bewildered Ragweed. "I had to run very fast to get away from that cat."

Clutch laughed. "Hey, mouse, you are seriously alien. Look, when I say cool, I mean, you know, like, it's good. Get it. Phat?"

"Fat?"

"That means *cool*, dude. Sweet."

"Oh, okay! Yes, thank you. I hope I am fat . . . sort of," Ragweed stammered. "Do you live here?"

"Yo, dude, this is my pad. I can think of other cars

I'd like better, but being on my own is my thing. Took what I could get. The freedom is worth it, mouse! Like, so sweet. My buds come, go. A few parties to lighten the load now and then, know what I'm saying? Mostly, though, just me, dude. I rip for liberty. Like, dude, I do what I do when I feel like doing it."

"And . . . and what exactly do you . . . do?" Ragweed asked.

"Hey, dude, I see it this way: Nothing happens in the world without noise. Know what I'm saying? So I'm a musician. Make the sound. Tickle the strings. Like, that's my axe over there, see?" Clutch nodded to the wooden spoon with threads on it that hung on the wall.

"I'm afraid I don't know what that is," Ragweed said.

Clutch gazed at him in wonderment. "It's a guitar, dude. Hey, like, you really must be some kind of Zeke."

"A what?"

"Never mind," Clutch said with a grin. "Like, there's two things I'm into. Music. You know, rock and roll. And the skateboard scene. I've got wheels and a way-down-funky band. We call ourselves the Be-Flat Tires. Pretty cool, don't you think? Actually, we're one short. I mean, Ragweed, I'm puffing serious about Silversides. Like, she chewed Muffler last week. Know what I'm saying? Said she didn't like his singing. Said only cats should do that. Makes me want to uncork my guts."

"Who was . . . Muffler?" Ragweed asked.

"Our lead singer. Hey, dude, can you sing?"

"I . . . I don't think so."

"Bummer. We could use another throat. Anyway, dude, you can crash here as long as you want to. Make yourself at home. Just be cool and keep one eye peeled for Silversides and other cats. Know what I'm saying?"

"I'm really not sure," Ragweed admitted.

"Well, anyway, you're in, dude. Like, give me four."

"Four what?"

"Four to the paw, mouse." Clutch held up her paw.

Ragweed reached out to shake it. Instead, Clutch slapped down on his paw, laughing. "Hey, mouse, I feel like I'm greeting Christopher Columbus. You know, welcome to the rest of the world, dude. Like, we're here. What took *you* so long?"

"I think I better get some sleep," Ragweed said. His head was swirling.

"Right, mellow out, kick back, chill and sleep in. Like, I do it all the time. But for now, I've got some things to do. Whatever. Just make sure you don't let Silversides in."

Ragweed looked around anxiously. "Will she try?"

"Hey, dude," Clutch went on, "that cat's serious bad news. That's why I have a bolt hole out back. But, like, if Silversides wants you out, dude, she's not going to rest till you're heading for heaven in an Indy Five Hundred. Know what I'm saying? Can you handle it? Take the heat with the chill?"

"I think so," Ragweed said, though he could not help wondering if it might not be wise—to save time and his life—to catch the next train right out of Amperville.

6

F.E.A.R.

Having failed to catch Ragweed, an angry, frustrated Silversides slunk home. There she hoped she would find some comfort, perhaps a chin stroke from a human, a fondle behind the ears.

Using her head to butt open the cat flap that had been installed at the back of the house, she went to the girl's room. The girl, however, would have nothing to do with her. Once again, a mouse—Blinker, this time—stood in Silversides's way.

There were times Silversides was convinced that if she could just get her claws into that horrid white rodent, much that was wrong in the world and her life would be made right. Unfortunately, the girl was too protective.

Telling herself she preferred to be left alone, Silversides took a few chews of the dry, gritty food bits in her bowl, lapped up two licks of stale water, then retreated to her bed by the furnace.

Though Silversides tried to settle down, she remained agitated. In her mind she kept seeing Ragweed pinned against the hole in the car. She knew she would have caught him, too, if some mouse had not interfered. All she saw of *that* mouse was the green fur on its head.

For the rest of the afternoon Silversides lay fuming on her rug. By early evening she was intensely restless, feeling a need to do *something* to calm her anger. Then she thought of Blinker, the white mouse upstairs. Maybe tonight she would be lucky enough to catch the vermin— or at least to torment him.

Rousing herself, the white cat crept to the top floor of the house by way of the back stairs. Stealthily she moved toward the girl's room. To her great joy the door had been left ajar.

A small shove, and Silversides slipped into the room. There she paused. Though the light was dim, her vision was good. Her sense of smell was better. The scent of mouse was overwhelming. Blinker was close. What a pleasure, thought Silversides, to nab him and drag him from the girl's room. It just had to be done quietly so no one would know what happened.

Treading lightly, Silversides let her nose guide her forward. Within moments she knew exactly where the white mouse was—on the girl's bed.

The cat rose up on her hind legs. Sure enough, there lay Blinker asleep on the pillow, a few inches from the girl's golden hair, the spot where Silversides used to sleep. The cat's wrath boiled.

Silently she sprang upon the bed, then slithered forward on her belly. A yard from the mouse, she tensed her rear legs and waggled her rump. After a count of three, she jumped. As she did, her rear foot scraped the girl's blanket.

That was enough sound for Blinker. His eyes popped

open. He saw the cat midair. Squeaking with terror, he dived for the protection of the girl's hair. The girl, disturbed, shifted her head.

Though Silversides knew she was going to miss the mouse, it was too late to hold back. When she came down, she landed right on the girl's face.

The girl screamed, sat up, grabbed the cat, and flung her away. Silversides, managing to twist about, landed on her feet and galloped from the room. As she raced down the hall, she heard the girl scream, "Keep out, you awful cat!"

In a rage even greater than usual Silversides tore out of the house. At first she had no thought where she was

going. Very soon, however, she veered toward Graybar's home. The vice president of F.E.A.R. lived a few city blocks away in a reeking old sewer. It took but moments to reach.

Graybar was eating from a pile of discarded chicken innards and bones. "Hey, pal," Graybar said when Silversides appeared. "Good timing. Eats."

"I'm not hungry," the white cat said. Food stolen from garbage was but one of Graybar's habits Silversides endured. "I'm mad."

"No big deal," Graybar sneered as he twitched a ragged ear. "You're always mad. What got you this time?"

Silversides recounted not only how she had failed to catch Ragweed but what happened regarding Blinker.

Graybar nodded with sympathy. "Ever notice that when these mice get away it's never on their own? Always depending on someone else. They gang up on us."

"They *are* vicious," Silversides agreed.

"Tell you what, though," Graybar said, crunching an old chicken legbone in two with his rear teeth. "I've got some good news."

"I need some."

"I found one of their clubs. They call it the Cheese Squeeze Club."

Silversides's gloom dropped away. Her claws tingled. "Where is it?"

"Down on Durham Street. Used to be a shoe-shine shop. How about you and me going over and brightening things up?"

"I'd love to," Silversides said.

"You're on, babe. Soon as I eat this chicken heart, we'll go get us some mice for dessert."

7
Blinker

linker, the white mouse who was the object of Silversides's rage, had been bred for laboratory research. His fur was pure white, his tail naked, his toes and nose pink. The slightest noise made him jump. The merest hint of danger brought fits of trembling. His eyes—so pink they looked bloodshot—could not bear bright light, a fact that caused him to blink a great deal.

Though he was a frail creature, life had treated Blinker relatively kindly. Instead of becoming part of an experiment, he had gone into a pet store. When still an infant he had been purchased by the girl who lived in Silversides's house. It was she who gave him his name.

The girl cared for Blinker a great deal. A cage complete with an exercise wheel was bought, along with a sack of the best mouse chow and a bottle of spring water. Sweet-smelling cedar chips lined his cage floor. The girl fed Blinker on schedule, never failing to provide fresh water or to change his cage chips regularly. When home from school she lavished affection on him, kissing and talking to him, carrying him about in her hands, on her shoulder, even in her pocket. She often brought him table scraps, candy, carrot bits, sugar cubes.

Though Blinker was supposed to live in the cage, the girl kept its door open. The only thing that the mouse was not allowed to do was leave the room.

"You are my blinky-winky mousey-wousey, and I don't want you gobbled up by that nasty-wasty cat," the girl crooned to the mouse. "So you must stay in our own room."

Blinker quickly learned the wisdom of this policy. Each encounter with Silversides proved dangerous. Not that Blinker ever learned why he was the object of so much hatred. It was simply a fact of life.

Since the girl went to school and was active in sports, Blinker spent most of his time alone. With the door to the room closed, he spent hours sitting by the window, gazing at the world beyond. To the young mouse, who had no experience other than the girl's room and his brief sojourn in the pet shop, the outside world was mysterious and appealing. Yet all he saw was a street, a park, other houses, humans, and many cars. Not once did he see another mouse.

Hardly a wonder, then, that Blinker came to believe that all mice—if there were any other mice—were like him: the same color, the same life, the same long, lonely hours staring out of windows from inside houses.

As time went by, Blinker wished the girl would allow him a taste of this outside world. She never did, not once.

There were moments Blinker felt a little peculiar about his desire to go beyond the room and the house. Perhaps, he told himself, this longing to explore was unnatural. Did he not have a life that included the freedom of the room and all the food he could eat, as well as a clean cage with an exercise wheel?

After all, he never saw other mice. Why should he want to go out? Full of guilt, he made himself do extra laps on the cage wheel by way of punishment. Between his desire and his guilt he kept slim, trim, and fit.

Then one day the girl made an announcement: "Blinker, I have to write a report for school, and I've decided to write about you. I need to explain all about mice and how you are the most special creature in the world."

Shortly afterward the girl brought home an armful of books. There was the *Oxford Illustrated History of Mice*, *Martha Stewart's Your House and Your Mouse*, and the *Book of World Mice*. There was fiction about mice, too, such as *The Story of a Bad Mouse*, *Runaway Ralph*, *Stuart Little*, *Abel's Island*, *Red Wall*, and others.

Blinker had never been much of a reader. The girl's books

usually held little interest for him. He avoided them except when he now and again would chew their bindings. In the current matter he had little choice. The girl not only read to him out loud, but she insisted he read by her side.

At first a reluctant reader, Blinker quickly became deeply absorbed in the books about mice. Long after the girl went to sleep he pored over them. When the girl was at school, he read even more.

These books altered Blinker's view of the world forever. He discovered that there were many kinds of mice, that most mice lived not in rooms but out in the world, that mice had families, that most of them lived free and independent lives. In short, to Blinker's utter astonishment, he discovered that the way *he* lived was the exception.

He went on to read everything in the girl's room he could get his paws on. In so doing he became highly educated.

This new knowledge made Blinker almost breathless with excitement. Now when he looked out the window, he saw things differently than before. The world, he realized, was something in which he might take part. He began to think he had a right to explore it, to make his

own decision as to where he lived. His freedom to go anywhere in the room was nothing more than the freedom to wander about a larger cage. Now he yearned to wander beyond the door, to be truly free.

Blinker was perfectly aware that there were moments when the door was left open. It was only a matter of time when that would occur again. When it did, he kept asking himself, should he or should he not escape? After all, there was the problem of Silversides. What was the point of freedom if it only led to death?

Everything changed for Blinker the night Silversides crept into the room, leaped onto the girl's bed, and almost caught him. When the girl chased Silversides from her room, she meant to slam the door shut. Being half asleep, she did not check to see if the door was truly closed.

After the attack, Blinker was too wide-eyed with fright to sleep. Instead, he prowled restlessly about the room. It took only a short time before he saw the door was open a crack. But anxious about Silversides's whereabouts, the mouse crept to the window and stared out into the world.

Moonlight illuminated the deserted street below. Trees appeared tall and majestic. The early spring flowers—daffodils and crocuses—seemed to glow.

Suddenly a white cat darted across the street. Blinker blinked. It was Silversides!

As Blinker watched the cat streak off, he suddenly realized he was free to leave the room. Just the thought of freedom made the white mouse tremble.

He glanced over his shoulder. The girl had gone back to sleep. Hardly thinking of what he was doing, Blinker leaped to the ground and scampered to the open door. In moments he was over the threshold.

Down the stairs he ran. At the bottom he began an almost

desperate search for a way to get outside. Unfortunately, every door was closed. So too were the windows. But what Blinker did find was the cat's entryway at the rear of the house.

Blinker was neither strong enough nor big enough to push this door open. But he was smart. Once he figured out how the cat door worked, he pushed it as if it were a swing, over and over again. Watching the door swing higher and higher, he set his movement for when the door was at its highest. Then he shot through, pulling his tail behind him with room to spare.

Blinker was outside . . . and free.

8

The Cheese Squeeze Club

An exhausted Ragweed slept all day. Once, twice he woke, found a few stale crumbs to nibble, then dropped back to sleep. He did not really open his eyes until Clutch woke him.

"Hey, dude, don't you think you've shaked enough?" she demanded.

"Is it morning?" Ragweed asked with a yawn.

"Mouse, you country dudes get here, the first thing you do is sleep for a week."

Ragweed sat up. "Did I sleep that much?"

"Hey, how about, like, all day? It's night already. You have anything in gear?"

"In gear?" Ragweed said as he got up slowly and stretched.

"Like, doing."

"I don't think so."

"Why not come over to my club with me?" Clutch suggested. "Catch my band. Meet some cool mice."

Ragweed sighed. "I'm afraid I don't know what a band or a club is," he admitted.

Clutch laughed. "You know what I like about you, dude?"

"No."

"Most dudes, when they don't know something, they're too frail to ask questions. Not you. You're a diesel, mouse. I mean, truly excellent. Okay. A band is a bunch of dudes playing music. And, like, a club is a place where friends meet. You know, some band music, and you can Mac out on crumbs and cheese. There's dancing, too. One sweet scene. We call it the Cheese Squeeze Club, and—"

"Clutch," Ragweed interrupted.

"What?"

"I . . . I don't know what *diesel, Mac out,* or *cheese* mean."

Openmouthed, Clutch stared at Ragweed for a long time. "You tugging me, dude?"

"I'm telling the truth."

"Awesome," the green-headed mouse murmured. "You are the whole thing plus chips. Okay. Like, a diesel is a motor, so, you know, powerful. *Mac out* means to eat. And cheese is . . . well . . . killer food. Trust me. It's made from milk. The point is, you hot to trot?"

"I guess."

"Only, remember what I told you before. Keep your eyes peeled for Silversides. We don't want to mess with her or her pal, Graybar. See, we keep the club like, secret. Don't want to have the cats find it. Know what I'm saying?"

"I think so."

Clutch removed her guitar from its place on the wall, then picked up a wafer of pale wood to which tiny wheels were attached front and back.

"What's that?" Ragweed asked.

"Like, basically, Ragweed," Clutch replied with a grin, "you are one played-out nerd. Know what I'm saying? It's my skateboard, dude. My wheels. Where you been?"

"In the country."

"Well, like, welcome to cementville." With care Clutch pulled aside the wood block that covered the entry to her car and peered out at the street. After carefully checking in all directions she said, "Cool. No cats."

As soon as the two mice stepped onto the sidewalk Clutch slid the wood piece over the hole behind her.

"In case you need to get in on your own," she said, "like, just give the wood a smack up here, dude." She banged along the top right corner. It popped open. "Otherwise it gets stuck," she added, closing the hole again.

Ragweed nodded.

"Let's hit it," Clutch said and dropped her skateboard to the ground. With one foot on the board and another on the ground—she was still holding her guitar—she pushed off. She had barely gone a few feet when she popped the board up—getting a lot of air, then coming down smoothly, if loudly, on the pavement, feet firmly planted on the deck. This was followed by a second jump, in which, midair, Clutch spun around so that when she landed she was facing Ragweed.

"Wow," he said, "that's . . . nice." He wanted to say "cool," but could not get it out.

"Called a one-eighty," Clutch explained with a grin as she did another half turn and sped off, but not before grinding loudly along the edge of a curb. Next moment she dropped off, did a maneuver high in the air—"An ollie, dude!"—then tore off again, using first one foot to ride, the other to shove, then reversing herself. Ragweed had to run to keep up.

As they went along Ragweed was able to gain a better sense of Amperville—or at least the section known as Mouse Town. It was too dark to see much, he reminded himself, and the lights on long poles were not very effective, but most of what he saw appeared to be very rundown. Human nests seemed abandoned. Windows were broken. Doors were shattered. The wide, dusty streets were littered with bits of paper, metal, wood. Abandoned cars were everywhere. The only thing living was straggly weeds growing through cracks in the pavement. Clearly, it had once been a busy place for humans, but no more.

After two more blocks, Clutch announced, "Here we are."

They had reached a small, broken-down building. A dilapidated sign reading "Sam's Shoe Shine" hung over a door frame without a door.

Clutch flipped her skateboard up and carried it over the threshold. Ragweed followed.

Whatever structure there was on the outside of the building, inside all had collapsed. Broken beams and cracked wallboard created a ceiling barely ten inches above the heads of the mice. Leading the way, Clutch moved right then left, then right again. "We keep it tight," she explained. "Like, to keep the cats out if they ever find it, which I seriously doubt."

At the end of the corridor the two mice scrambled through a hole in the wall, entering an open area with a ceiling made of rusty screening. At the other side of the area was a counter. Behind it stood an enormously fat mouse with large ears, brown fur, and a scaly tail. He was offering up cracker crumbs and cheese to those who asked.

"Mayor of Mouse Town," Clutch said, with a nod to the mouse. "Goes by the name of Radiator."

The area was alive with mice of many colors, shapes, and sizes. Ragweed noticed a few golden mice, some deer mice, a few short-tailed grasshopper mice, lots of house mice—like Clutch—even an occasional meadow-jumping mouse. Ragweed had never seen so many different kinds of mice in one place.

A few were alone. Most, however, were in groups about small piles of crumbs and cheese. Talk—loud, constant squeaking—made it hard to hear.

"Hey, mouse, over here," Clutch shouted over the din to Ragweed. "Meet my band buds."

Clutch threaded her way through the crowd. "Hey, dude," mice called to her. "What's happening?" "What's up?" "Hey, sweetheart!"

In contrast, Ragweed bumped his way through the mice. "Excuse me. Sorry. Pardon. I do beg your pardon. Thanks." Under the stares of the mice, he felt very much the outsider.

"Hey, dudes, what's up?" Clutch cried. She had reached the far corner of the room. Two very different mice were sitting about a small pile of crumbs. "This is my new bud, Ragweed," she announced. "Just trickled into town."

The two mice looked up casually. Their faces showed no emotion.

"This is Dipstick," Clutch went on. "One big bad drummer. He's a grasshopper mouse."

"Whatever," Dipstick murmured with a nod of his head. He had cinnamon-colored fur on his back, a white belly, and a white-tipped tail.

"And this dude is Lugnut," Clutch continued. "Pygmy mouse."

Gray-brown in color, Lugnut was half the size of Ragweed, with tiny, delicate paws. His lidded eyes made him appear very sleepy. "He's on the bass," Clutch explained. "Awesome noise."

"What's up, dude?" Lugnut said to Ragweed in a soft drawl.

"I'm very pleased to meet you both," Ragweed said.

"Yo, mouse, whatever," Dipstick said. "Hunker down and toss a crumb." He gestured to the pile.

"Thank you." Ragweed sat down and out of politeness took a bit.

"When's our set?" Clutch asked.

"Soon."

After a moment, Ragweed said, "What's a set?"

Dipstick rolled his eyes. Lugnut darted an unbelieving glance at Ragweed, then at Clutch.

"Hey, like," she said, "he just blew into town."

"Yeah, right," Lugnut murmured. "A set is our performance," he explained to Ragweed. "Ten, twelve tunes. We do three sets a night."

Dipstick hopped up. "Anyone want something to drink?"

Clutch looked at Ragweed. "What do they have?" Ragweed asked.

"Nectar. Honey. Water."

"Water, thank you."

"Anyone else?"

The other mice shook their heads. Dipstick went off.

Ragweed watched the crowd. Most of the mice seemed to be arguing, yet without anger. He wondered that there was so much to talk about. Then it dawned on him: these mice *enjoyed* squeaking at one another. He found it fascinating.

Clutch leaned over to Lugnut. "This dude here," she indicated Ragweed, "gets off the train and, like, who do you think is waiting to say hello?"

Lugnut gazed at Ragweed. "Graybar? Silversides?"

Clutch nodded.

"Busted," Lugnut muttered.

Dipstick came back with a bottle cap filled with water in one paw. He gave it to Ragweed. "Radiator says we're on," he announced.

Clutch and Lugnut heaved themselves up. "Enjoy the sound," Clutch said. "Keep an eye on my deck, will you?"

"Deck?" Ragweed asked.

"Skateboard."

"Oh, sure."

Lugnut shook his head in disbelief as the trio eased their way through the crowd. Ragweed heard him say, "Your dude's an airhead."

"Hey, like, he's funky," Clutch returned.

"Yeah, right," Dipstick said.

Ragweed sighed, drew in the skateboard, took a sip of water, then settled in to watch. For a moment he lost sight of his new friends, only to see them reappear on the far side of the room on what looked like a small platform.

Dipstick seated himself amid a number of small tuna-fish cans. Lugnut carried a large guitar made from a red plastic spoon and string. His guitar was bigger than the one Clutch had and made the tiny mouse seem even smaller than he was. As for Clutch, she was in front of the other two, tuning her own guitar.

Radiator, who had been behind the counter, waddled to the platform. "Okay, guys," he called out to the crowd. "Glad you could make it down here tonight to the Cheese Squeeze Club. Our house band, the Be-Flat Tires, is going to do a set. How about giving these cool dudes some Cheese Squeeze Club paw!"

Some ragged applause and a few squeaks were heard.

Clutch stepped forward. "How you dudes doing?"

"Want some funk!" came a reply.

"Okay!" Clutch continued. "We're one short tonight. Sorry to tell you, but Silversides gaffled Muffler."

Moans and groans rose from the crowd.

Clutch continued. "Hey, no one said being a mouse is easy. Nothing we can do about it but keep on trucking. That's the way Muffler would have wanted it. Right? Right! So, like, let's get into some sweet Be-Flat Tires grooves. Anyway, we're dedicating tonight's show to Muffler. Okay." She turned to her band and nodded her green head. "One, two, three . . ."

The music began.

Ragweed was astonished. He had never heard such sounds before. There was a heavy, repetitious beat from Dipstick, who was flailing away on the tin cans with some twigs, making an awful racket. Every now and again, on a particularly strong beat, he leaped straight up in the air, high above his drums. Tiny Lugnut, all but hidden behind his red guitar, nodded to the beat, closed his eyes, and plucked the strings with great intensity as his tail lashed about wildly. As for Clutch, she bobbed her green-tinted head and bounced up and down as she played. Her earring swung as her tail kept to the rhythm. Then in a hoarse voice she broke into song:

"Mouse in a box
Thinks he's a fox,
But he's just full of rage
living on life's lousy wage.
'Cause the world ain't cheese
And can't say please!
Hey, nothing is a snap.
Look out, here comes the trap!

'*Cause the world ain't cheese*
And can't say please!
'*Cause the world ain't cheese*
And can't say please!
Look out, dudes, here comes the trap!''

The last line was repeated over and over again, with Dipstick and Lugnut joining in from time to time with their own close harmony.

Meanwhile, out on the floor, a fair number of mice had gotten up and started to dance. They were gyrating, some holding their paws up while they were turning, twisting, dipping, shaking, and hopping, with tails lashing about. Some mice even leaped straight up into the air above the crowd, squeaking and squealing as they came down.

And yet, as Ragweed looked on, there was hardly a smile in the crowd. The dancers didn't look at one another, but appeared to be more deeply involved in the music than aware of their partners. Some had their eyes closed. Others stared fixedly up at the screen above or at their feet.

As Clutch sang on, Ragweed found himself timidly tapping out the beat with his toes.

Suddenly there was an enormous crash. The startled musicians stopped playing. The dancing ceased. Every mouse in the club turned in the direction of the noise. For a moment all was still. Then one of the club walls collapsed. Into the room burst Silversides's face.

"Good evening, mice," she said, grinning so that all her teeth were visible. "F.E.A.R. is here."

9

What Happened at the Cheese Squeeze Club

The mice stared in horror at Silversides's face. The next moment, when the opposite wall fell in and Graybar's eyes and whiskers appeared, chaos erupted.

The club was filled with squeaking, screaming, running, hopping, leaping mice, rushing as one toward the single available exit. But the opening was far too narrow to accommodate the crush. Mice were pushed, shoved, and trampled. Only a few managed to escape.

When the remaining mice tried to find another way out, they were confronted by the two cats calling out, "Cats rule! Mice out! Rodents retreat! Felines first!"

At first Ragweed was too bewildered to do anything but gape at the wild confusion before him. But when Graybar leaped into the middle of the milling mice and began pouncing and biting, a terrified Ragweed shrank back into a corner.

From there he looked toward the platform where the Be-Flat Tires had been playing. Dipstick was leaping straight up and down, squeaking raucous insults at the cats. Lugnut crouched behind his bass guitar as if it were a shield against possible attack. As for Clutch, she was holding her guitar by its neck, clearly willing to use it as a weapon. The look upon her face was nothing less than ferocious.

Two cats. Forty-five mice. Despite their numbers, the mice, overwhelmed by both the suddenness and ruthlessness of the cats' attack, put up very little resistance. Instead they tried desperately to get away. The two cats, grinning and howling with glee, were catching and tossing mice about at will. One blow of a cat's paw, and another poor mouse was either laid low or tossed across the room like a bean bag.

Not all the mice were so passive. When Clutch saw Silversides step on a young mouse's tail and gradually draw her victim in, as if reeling in a fish, she leaped from the performance platform and, bent on rescue, dashed forward. Coming close to the cat, she hauled back her guitar and swung with all her might, smacking Silversides right on her nose. There was a loud *plunk*. The guitar strings snapped. The guitar shattered.

Taken by surprise, Silversides removed her paw from her victim's tail and touched her nose to see if anything had broken. The freed mouse leaped away and was lost in the crowd.

Surprised as well as smarting, the white cat searched for her attacker. She did not have to look far. An irate Clutch stood before her, holding the fragmented instrument in her paws.

"Hey, you thick dude, why don't you trash someone your own size!" she screamed with no apparent thought

for her own safety. "Like, we've got just as much right to be here as you do! Know what I'm saying?"

"No, I don't know what you're saying, you vulgar-mouthed vermin," Silversides retorted. Shooting out a paw she smacked Clutch broadside, hurling the green-headed mouse back up against a wall. Clutch hit hard, slid to the floor, and lay motionless, eyes closed. Only her earring was moving, swinging back and forth like a pendulum.

Ragweed—who had seen it all—gasped. He was sure Clutch had been killed.

Silversides seemed to think otherwise. Gathering herself up, she prepared to leap upon the mouse and deliver a finishing blow.

Clutch shook her head groggily and opened her eyes.

She made an effort to rise but was apparently incapable of getting up. Silversides was grinning at her, ready to spring.

One moment Ragweed was relieved to see that Clutch was alive. The next moment he saw what was about to happen and was appalled. Barely thinking, he snatched up Clutch's skateboard and ran to his new friend's side.

Silversides, mouth open so wide her gullet was fully exposed, took a flying leap at Clutch. Ragweed lifted the skateboard over his head to protect himself and his friend. Down came Silversides, mouth wide. Feeling her hot breath on his ears, Ragweed shoved the skateboard into the cat's mouth. The cat tried to close her jaws, but could not. Her mouth was wedged open by the skateboard.

Taken by surprise, the cat uttered a throaty shriek and rolled over on her back. Kicking desperately, she tried to get the board out of her mouth. It stayed stuck.

Across the room, Graybar looked around and saw Silversides writhing about on the floor. Momentarily forgetting the brawl, he limped over to his companion. "Hey, babe, what's the matter?" he asked her. "What are you saying?"

"I . . . outh . . . uck," was all Silversides could manage.

Not understanding what had happened, Graybar just laughed.

"I . . . outh . . . uck!" Silversides shrieked.

Finally Graybar understood. He knelt and tried to pry the skateboard from his friend's mouth.

Seeing that the cats were occupied, Ragweed snatched one of Clutch's paws and gave a yank. "Come on," he cried, "run for it!"

Clutch staggered to her feet. Led by Ragweed, the two pushed their way through the mob of mice who were trying frantically to get out of the room. Fortunately, the walls smashed by the cats provided new avenues for escape. Mice were streaming away to safety.

Dragging the dazed Clutch after him, Ragweed plunged through one of the holes in the walls.

10

Blinker, Continued

I n another part of Amperville the full moon was high, the night air soft, the fragrances of spring rich and varied. Blinker's pink nose, framed by his fine, fair whiskers, trembled and his pink eyes kept blinking as he tried to take in a world so very much bigger than the room he knew.

"Oh, my," he prattled in a daze of happy wonderment. "So many *sounds* . . . So many *smells* . . . So much to *see!*" Like an unsure compass needle, he turned round and round on shaky legs until he grew dizzy.

Stopping and starting, he made his way across the lawn in front of his house. The grass tickled his feet so, he had to pause more than once because of uncontrollable giggling. Here and there he plunged his nose into the ground and inhaled the sweet and musky smell—only to get a snootful of dirt and dust, which caused him to sneeze repeatedly. "It's all so—ah-choo!—amazing," he wheezed. "So delight—ah-choo!—ful!"

In a moment of abandon, he rolled over in the grass

and kicked his pink feet in the air, which gave him the sensation that he was walking on the moon. Another kick righted him and he began to run about wildly.

When he reached the sidewalk in front of his house, he put a paw on the concrete. "Goodness, this is *hard*," he murmured, almost as if he were learning a new language. "Yet very *cool*. Delightfully so. It is. It really is."

He continued along the sidewalk, poking his nose this way and that. Every few inches he reared up on his hind legs and gazed about. "Oh!" he cried in rapture. "My shadow by moonlight. How velvety, how . . . mysterious."

When Blinker reached the curb, he gazed down into the gutter where puddles had gathered. "Why, I believe that's *water*! But not in a bottle or a glass. It's just *free*!" He studied the water so intently, he leaned over too far and tumbled head over heels, landing with a splat in the middle of a puddle.

Thoroughly soaked, Blinker sat up, grimaced, looked around, then began to laugh uncontrollably. "Ridiculous. I mean, I am . . . so helpless. Like an infant. That's what I am. A perfect baby! I might as well be blind and naked. It's all so silly, but wonder—" He could not finish his sentence. He was laughing too hard. Dripping wet, he eased himself out of the water and began to move across the road.

Unexpectedly, there was an explosion of light so bright he was blinded. Then Blinker heard a roar louder than anything he had ever before heard in his life. Unable to see, to move, much less to think, he went numb with terror. The next moment the machine that made the roar hurtled over him, missing him with just inches to spare, creating a wind that left him frightened and coughing.

"What was *that*?" Blinker asked himself as he looked

in the direction the thing had gone. All he saw were receding red lights. "A car," he said to himself in a shaky voice. "I forgot about cars." He pressed both front paws over his wildly beating heart. "I could get . . . killed."

In haste, Blinker retreated to the gutter and attempted to climb the curb, which proved too high and smooth to manage. Given no choice, Blinker scampered the length of the gutter. When he reached the end of the block he halted. He knew he wanted to go home. An inner voice scolded him for being weak while urging him to be bold, to continue on, to explore the world.

In the end, Blinker compromised between urges: He would go on and see as much as he could by night. But as soon as daylight came, he would return to the house and the safety of his room.

Having calmed himself with this self-imposed limit, Blinker ventured upon the street again. This time he carefully checked both ways for any sign of danger before proceeding. Only when he was certain there was none did he dart across the street and into a park.

He took time to feel the rough bark of the massive trees. When he came upon a flower, a lily of the valley, he almost swooned with delight at its strong fragrance and delicate white bells.

Blinker went on, drawn by one astonishing discovery after another. First it was a damp, wiggling worm. Then a pinecone. A shiny pebble seemed to have captured the light of the moon on its smooth surface. There were signs of humans, too: ash cans, piles of newspaper, benches. It was as if each thing he came upon was the rarest of marvels and he the first to find it. "Truly remarkable," he kept whispering. "Truly, truly, truly."

Only after he had gone on for a long time did Blinker

happen to look up: The darkness was fading. In its place was soft, gray light. Wondering, he stared at it. "Goodness," he sighed, "even the sky changes." Then he remembered his promise to himself: It was time to return home.

Regretfully, but with some relief, Blinker turned about, only to realize he had neglected to keep track of his route. He had no idea where he was, much less how to get back home.

Eyes squinting, tail twitching, he looked around. What had seemed very beautiful moments before had become a bewildering maze.

He darted off in one direction, certain he had come from that way. The next moment he felt sure it was not from that way, but from this. Trembling with fear, he came to a stop. He was lost.

"Get a grip on yourself, Blinker," he murmured and made himself look around in the growing morning light.

He was on a sidewalk. The buildings—at least compared with houses in his own neighborhood—were not as brightly painted. Some windows were broken. Doors were lopsided. Many more cars went by than in the night, terrifying in their size, noise, and smell.

As Blinker pondered his difficulty he heard a strange sound. He had not the least idea what this long, high-pitched, drawn-out whistle might be. Still, it was something.

"I must get back home," he told himself and crept along, halting every few feet to rise up on his hind legs and look and sniff, hoping that every corner he turned would reveal something familiar. None did, and in his confusion the whistle drew him like a beacon of light.

11
Windshield and Foglight

Safely beyond the ruins of the Cheese Squeeze Club, Ragweed halted. "Are you all right?" he asked Clutch.

Clutch shook her head clear, then looked back toward the club. "Oh, mouse, why do those cats hate us so much?" she cried. Tears ran down her cheeks. "Like, what did we ever do to them? Know what I'm saying? They're so big and powerful. And what can we do? Like, zippo."

Ragweed did not know what to say.

Taking a deep breath, Clutch wiped away tears. "Hey, dude, you were something else. You saved my life. I mean, you were totally awesome."

"You saved mine before," Ragweed said. "So we're even. Except I don't think we should stand here, talking. We need to find a safer place. You sure you're okay?"

"Hey, I'm cool," Clutch said. But suddenly she turned to look again at what had been the club. "Hey, like, what about Dipstick and Lugnut? Have you seen them?"

"I'm afraid not."

Clutch swallowed hard. "What about my guitar?" she asked.

"You smashed it on Silversides's nose."

"Oh, yeah, right. And my deck?"

"In Silversides's mouth."

Clutch put her paws over her eyes. "Total yard sale," she said. "Biffed."

Ragweed touched Clutch's shoulder gently. "Ah . . . dude," he said tentatively, "you did the best you could."

"Yeah, like, maybe," Clutch replied. Suddenly she grinned. "Hey, was that some kind of killer music or what? Right on the cat's nose leather." Just as quickly she became grim again. "Do you think my buds got, like, planted deep?"

"I don't know."

"Oh, mouse, the Cheese Squeeze Club was one cool place. Know what I'm saying? Maybe I should go back and check on my buds."

"Clutch," Ragweed urged, "like, don't you think we'd be safer somewhere else?"

"Safe? Yeah, right. We better haul. Follow me."

As the two mice scurried along the sidewalk, Ragweed noticed they were not going back the way they had come. "Aren't we going the wrong way?" he asked.

"Not really. Like, it might not be safe to go back to my pad right away. Can't tell. Maybe Silversides knows where it's at. That's where she chased you. I mean, to live around here, dude, you have to have street savvy."

"Street savvy?"

"Like, keep your mind to the bind and your feet to the beat. Know what I'm saying?"

"I think so. Where are we going?"

"To my old mouse's place. They'll let us hang till this blows over. It's not far."

After a two-block run Clutch darted into an alleyway and squirmed under a metal wall whose lower edge was old rubber.

On the other side of the wall stood a very long and, to Ragweed's eyes, immense metal box with a long row of dirty windows. The box was perched on flat tires and painted yellow, though the paint was peeling badly. On one side of the box was written "Amperville School District."

"What is that?" Ragweed said.

"Old school bus, dude. Where my parents hang out their tails."

Ragweed, who had no idea what a school bus was, decided it was not the moment to ask more questions. Instead, he followed Clutch up into the bus itself.

At the top of the ramp Clutch paused. "My folks are way cool, mouse. Just be yourself. You'll do fine."

Inside the bus the walls were covered with pictures painted on bits of paper with chewed edges.

"Oh, my," Ragweed murmured.

"Like, my old mouse is an artist," Clutch said with pride. "Know what I'm saying?" She stopped so Ragweed could admire the work.

At first Ragweed thought it was the dimness of the bus that made it difficult to see the pictures clearly. Then he realized it was not the light but the art that was obscure. The pictures consisted mainly of swirls of color and curious shapes. He could not begin to tell what they represented, if anything.

"The old mouse—his name is Windshield, but we call

him Windy—is really into cheese," Clutch explained. "That's what he paints."

"He paints *cheese?*" Ragweed asked, bewildered.

"Hey, duh, not the cheese itself. Like, he does *portraits* of cheese. Know what I'm saying? See, here, that's his famous *Yellow Cheese Descending a Stairway.* This one is from his Blue Cheese period. Over there is *American Cheese.* That blank picture isn't really blank. It's a hole from some Swiss cheese. I mean, killer amazing. It takes, like, one wicked mind to think of nothing, don't you think? I bet you can never guess how Windy does it?"

"No, I don't think I could," Ragweed admitted.

"Uses his tail. Like, he may be my old mouse," Clutch said with pride, "but the guy's an awesome genius."

"Does your mother paint too?" Ragweed asked.

"Foglight?" Clutch said. "Naw, she's a poet. She's writing a mouse epic. Calls it *Cheese of Grass*. Going to be killer sweet. Word wipeout time. Been working on it for weeks. Should be done any sec now. But, hey, dude, let me introduce you to them."

They passed down the center of the bus between rows of broken seats. Pictures hung everywhere. Some, Ragweed saw at a glance, were cheese paintings and presumably had been painted by Clutch's father. But there were other paintings: portraits of mice, landscapes, visions of human nests, streets. There were also twisted objects of all kinds. Ragweed was reminded of the pile of junk in which he had hidden by the railroad.

"My folks have a lot of artist friends," Clutch whispered by way of explanation. "They can't sell what they

make, so they swap stuff. Hey, Windy! Foggy! What's up?"
Clutch called.

At the front of the old bus were two mice. The large
one—Ragweed guessed he was Clutch's father, the one
called Windshield—was quite portly. His scruffy fur was
gray-brown like his daughter's, but so dabbed with color
he looked like a spotted creature. All around him was an
array of bottle caps, each filled with paint of a different
color. The tip of his tail—he was in the middle of painting
a picture—was quite green. Ragweed noticed it was the
same color as the top of Clutch's head.

The other mouse, who was small and wiry, was bend-
ing intently over the work she was composing on paper,
chewing a writing stick. Though Clutch called a greeting,
she seemed not to have heard.

Not so with Clutch's father. He looked around.
"Clutch!" he rumbled in as low a voice as Ragweed had
ever heard. "What a magnificent surprise!" He bounded
forward and gave his daughter an enthusiastic nuzzle,
which she returned with equal fervor.

"Hey, Windy," Clutch said, "this is my new bud, Ragweed. He just blew into town, and like, he already saved
my life."

"Saved your life?" the fat mouse cried, eyes sparking
with interest. "Sir," he exclaimed, "I should like to shake
your paw." He did so with great vigor and enthusiasm. "It
is clear, young mouse, you subscribe to the same philosophy as I do, the world of big gestures! Action! Commit-
ment!" He clung to Ragweed's paw, continuing to shake
it. "I'm delighted to meet you! No, correction! *Thrilled* to
meet you! Welcome to the family," he went on, all the
while pumping Ragweed's paw.

"Oh, well, thank you," Ragweed said mildly.

"Did you hear, Foggy?" Windshield cried, turning toward his wife. "This delightful young mouse saved our daughter's life!"

"That's nice," Clutch's mother said. "Be finished in two secs." Though she seemed to mean it, she was too intent upon her work to break off.

Not so Windshield. "Come on over here, you two. Great to see you, Clutch. Love your hair! You know," he said, suddenly halting and rising up on his hind legs, as if giving a sermon, "when a stranger saves the life of another stranger—it seems to me that we have reached a major turning point. It means mice are beginning to take care of mice.

"It's a trend!" he cried with great sweeping motions of one paw. "What has happened will affect other mice. They will affect yet others. The movement will spread and the whole world of mice will change! It's a revolution!"

"Windy," Clutch said, "like, can we get something to eat?"

"Of course," Windshield said good-naturedly. "Foggy," he called to his wife, "care to join us?"

"Just two secs," Foglight mumbled again without looking up.

"My wife," Windshield explained to Ragweed with pride, "is a wonderful writer. Do you know how you can tell a professional writer from an amateur?"

"No."

"An amateur worries about the work before starting; a professional worries about the work when finished."

Windshield led the two young mice under a seat, where food was piled about in random fashion. "Help yourself, my dear friends. Now then, Ragweed, the complete story. No detail is too small. How did you preserve my daughter's life? I desire to hear it all."

"It was at the Cheese Squeeze Club—" Ragweed began.

"The Cheese Squeeze Club," Windshield interrupted. "These places where young people congregate are important. When I was young, it was different. We were isolated. Today a whole new feeling has emerged. A sense of belonging. And these clubs mark a turning point! A trend! The world is changing! Revolution is at hand!"

"Windy," Clutch interrupted, "do you want to know what happened?"

"Certainly."

"Silversides and Graybar mopped up the club."

"Cruel, hateful creatures," Windshield cried. "Holding down the mice of this town! Repressing us. But our time will come." He clenched a paw and held it high. "We mice shall rise again!"

"Like, tell me about it," Clutch said.

"Never give up heart," Windshield proclaimed. "Remember, we're at a turning point. Notice that a whole new feeling has emerged. A new sense of belonging. A revolution!"

"Hey, Pops," Clutch said with affection, "like, you've said that already."

"I have?" The artist was truly surprised.

"At least."

"Oh, well, repetition is the proof of sincerity. Saying what you mean is important. It's a turning point. A whole new—"

"Windy!" Clutch cried, cutting him off.

Then Ragweed said, "Mr. Windshield, sir, do you think anything can be done about the cats? Like, make them stop hurting you guys?"

Windshield seemed to deflate. "Well, if you put it that

way, no. But, young fellow, the power of art will—" He stopped mid-sentence. "That reminds me," he said. He rushed out from under the seat, headed for the back of the bus, and resumed painting.

Ragweed looked to Clutch. "Like, the power of art will *what?*" he asked her.

"Beats me," Clutch said, laughing. "That's the way the dude always talks. He's, like, constantly cruising. Dreaming. Except, know what I'm saying, most of his dreams come when he's awake."

"Clutch," Ragweed said, "really, isn't there, like, anything to be done about those cats?"

Clutch sighed. "Hey, dude, I'll tell it like it is. There are us mice, okay, and then there are those cats. We don't deserve it, but they hate us. Generally speaking, we lose. Totally. Hey, it's what's going down. A constant struggle. And that's the way it's going to be."

"But," Ragweed stammered, "that's an awful way to live."

"Hey, dude, you've been here what, one day? Two? Right? Me, I've spent my whole life looking over both my shoulders for cats. So chill. Know what I'm saying? Keep on living till we die. No other way. It'll come. And there's nothing we can do about it. But hey, baby, you live with regrets, you'll wind up regretting living."

12
Silversides

Though Silversides was satisfied by the havoc she and Graybar had wreaked on the Cheese Squeeze Club, it left a distinctly bad taste in her mouth. Of course she *had* bitten down hard on that mouse's skateboard, the one the golden mouse had rammed into her mouth. That part of the evening had been a painful and humiliating experience.

Graybar had rescued Silversides by carefully working the board out of her mouth. The vice-president of F.E.A.R. thought it all very funny. "Are you telling me you let a *mouse* stick that board into your mouth and you didn't bite him in half?" he asked, not bothering to conceal his amusement.

"I didn't see it until it was too late," Silversides tried to explain. "I was trying to get a green-headed mouse."

"A green-headed mouse! You should look before you bite," Graybar suggested with a smirk.

"Easy for you to say," Silversides retorted.

"Who was the mouse who stuck it to you?" Graybar asked.

"Some golden mouse."

"Golden mouse? Not the one you missed grabbing this morning, was it?"

Silversides frowned. "Yes," she said.

"You should have tossed him when you had the chance, cat," Graybar said with a laugh. "You better deal with him."

Silversides, telling herself that she had to stop working with Graybar, said, "Don't worry, I will."

The mice had all fled, so there was little for the cats to do other than complete their systematic destruction of the club. This they did with grim satisfaction, making sure that the establishment could never be restored.

"Got any plans for tomorrow?" Graybar asked Silversides before they parted on the street.

"I've got some things to do," Silversides said by way of excusing herself. The truth was, she wanted some time to think.

"Going for the green and gold?" Graybar smirked.

Instead of answering, Silversides turned and, her tail stiff, set off.

"Catch you later," Graybar cried after her.

Sore-mouthed and weary, ready for sleep, Silversides eased herself up into her home through the back entry flap. But no sooner did she get into the house than she came to a stop. The air was filled with an unusual aroma. It took just moments to figure out what it was: mouse. While she had been out, a mouse had come into the house! The mere thought of it rekindled her anger.

Furious, the cat took a few more deep whiffs. That enabled her to make an even more important discovery: the mouse scent belonged to *Blinker*!

The meaning was clear. The hated mouse had left the

girl's room. If Blinker was still out and about he would be defenseless. A surge of excitement gripped Silversides. Revenge was at paw. Her exhaustion fell away.

Quickly, quietly, and efficiently, Silversides stalked the house. She examined every room, every hallway, every closet. Gradually the trail took her to the girl's room. Though the door was open, a check of the room proved fruitless.

Puzzled, Silversides reversed direction, following Blinker's scent the other way, from the girl's room to the cat door at the back of the house and then out into the backyard. The evidence was as clear as it was remarkable: Blinker must have left the house.

"The wretched creature has fled," the cat thought with glee. "Victory is mine!"

Going to her rug bed, Silversides allowed herself a long, luxurious stretch and a flex of claws. Her purr was deep.

The night, after all, had been proven extraordinarily successful. It was so successful the future finally looked bright. Life in the house would return to normal. She and the girl would become friends again. Satisfaction would return. Silversides yawned with pleasure, only to feel the pain in her mouth.

The pain turned Silversides's thoughts to the golden mouse, the one who had humiliated her twice. Yes, and the green-headed one. If she could get rid of those two, the good old times would be completely restored.

The cat stretched again, yawned, and licked herself until, drowsy with the repetitious monotony of it all, she fell into a deep slumber.

"What have you done with my darling mouse!"

Silversides woke with a start. It was morning. The girl

was holding her in midair by the scruff of the neck. Her face was angry and streaked with tears.

"You naughty thing!" the girl shouted at Silversides. "You've done something horrible to my sweet Blinker. I know you have. Where is he?" she demanded.

Silversides, dangling helplessly in the girl's grip, stared with wrath at the human. Human faces were generally repulsive to Silversides—so utterly hairless, so emotional, so without dignity. There was no way the white cat was going to tell the girl anything.

"What did you do?" the girl raged on. "Tell me!"

It was all that Silversides—who wished she *had* done something to Blinker—could do to keep from hissing at the girl.

"You must find him," the girl demanded shrilly, "even if it's only his poor, broken body. Bring him to me. Do you understand, you naughty cat? I want him home dead or alive, or you are not welcome here anymore!"

"Oh, you are so stupid!" the girl cried when Silversides refused to respond, not so much as a meow.

"You wretched cat!" The girl burst into tears. "Don't you dare come back unless you bring Blinker!" She flung Silversides into the backyard and slammed the door shut.

Silversides stared at the house. Her bitterness was as deep as it was intense. She looked about. It was early morning. A slight breeze was blowing from the west. She lifted her nose and sniffed deeply. Amid the countless smells she could just detect Blinker's scent. She tried to untangle his odor from the others. When it came it was like one thread pulled from a knotted ball of twine.

It was enough. She would be able to follow the white mouse's trail and find him. When she caught up with him she would kill him and bring his mangled body back just

as the girl had asked her to. Then she'd search out that golden mouse and the green-headed one and deal with them, too.

Nose to the ground, Silversides began to follow Blinker's faint but unmistakable trail.

13
Ragweed Wanders

Though Ragweed woke up in the old bus quite early, Windshield was already working hard on his painting. The stout mouse, lost in thought, spent long periods of time staring at his work. During these times he hardly moved except to glance at his caps of paint, then back at his work. It was as if he were painting the picture in his mind. Then he would burst into a fury of activity, dipping his tail into first one bottle cap, then another, all but throwing the paint onto the picture with wild abandon.

Not too long afterward, Dipstick and Lugnut appeared. Clutch was roused from her sleep to greet them.

The three members of the Be-Flat Tires embraced warmly. "Hey, dudes," Clutch cried. "You made it. Far out. Cool. Killer cool."

"I'm glad to be alive," Dipstick said. "I mean, those cats turned off, like, twenty dudes."

"Oh, mouse," Clutch cried. "Totally nasty."

"And the club's wasted. Knocked out of town. What was ain't no more."

"Lost my bass," Lugnut added in his sleepy way. "Dipstick lost his drums. What about your guitar?"

"Blew apart on Silversides's nose," Clutch said. "My deck, too." She told her friends how Ragweed used her skateboard to save her.

"Awesome, dude," they both murmured. Considering Ragweed with new respect, both put up their paws to slap. Ragweed was pleased.

"But, bummer, dudes," Dipstick said, "now we've got no place to play."

The band members looked at one another and nodded sadly. "Awesome ugly," Lugnut said.

"Way down," Dipstick agreed.

There was a moment of silence. Then Clutch brightened. "Hey, dudes, how about some chow?"

"Yo, mouse," Lugnut agreed. "I could eat a cat." The three mice went looking for food. Ragweed held back. He had the feeling he was intruding, that the three band members needed to be together without him.

He was still hesitating when Windshield came up to his side. "Wonderful how the band stays together, isn't it?" the artist said enthusiastically, nodding in the direction of the trio. "As I see it, young mouse," he went on, "it represents a whole new trend! Mice sticking together in the face of . . . That reminds me . . ." He rushed back to his painting.

Ragweed wandered about the dilapidated bus. When he came upon Clutch's mother, Foglight appeared not to have moved since he first had seen her. She was still hunched over her work, her writing stick chewed to a nub.

She looked up at Ragweed, puzzlement in her eyes. "Are you a friend of Clutch's?" she asked.

"Well, like, actually, yes," Ragweed replied. "I came yesterday and . . . you and I were introduced."

"Clutch has so many friends," Foglight said, though there was no recognition in her eyes. "Do you know a good word for *brave?*"

"*Fearless?*" Ragweed said gravely.

"That'll be the day," Foglight murmured and went back to pondering her writing.

Feeling completely at sixes and sevens, Ragweed returned to where the three mice were eating and talking. "Hey, dudes, I think I'll go."

"Catch you at my pad," Clutch called after him.

Ragweed, who gladly would have changed his plans if his new friend had asked him to join the threesome, gave a casual wave and made his way out of the nest.

Once outside, he squinted at the bright sun. He had

almost forgotten about daylight. The thought brought an unexpected wave of homesickness. At the Brook, one was always aware of the time of day. In the city, apparently, daylight came as a surprise. "It *is* different here," Ragweed murmured to himself without much enthusiasm.

With no particular desire to return to Clutch's place without her, he crept along the sidewalks, keeping close to the bases of walls and old human nests. From time to time he would dart forward, pause, and sit up to look about, mainly checking for cats. Seeing none, he continued on, heading no place in particular, just wandering aimlessly.

The size of the human nests awed him. They appeared to him almost as big as the sky. When cars tore by, emitting smoke, fumes, and noise, he was terribly frightened. Clearly, such contraptions were to be avoided at all costs. But there were so many of them.

From time to time Ragweed saw humans, too. Though also huge, they generally paid no attention to him. There

were moments when Ragweed wondered if they even saw him. But when a human finally did notice him, the person stopped, uttered something like a gasp, and moved around Ragweed in a wide circle.

"This city certainly doesn't like mice," Ragweed murmured to himself.

Still, what did impress him about the city was the endless variety of things to be seen. The range of color was extraordinary, rather like one of Windshield's paintings—shapes and colors that were endlessly fascinating. Equally engrossing to him was the angularity of everything. In the country, one rarely saw a straight line. Even the tallest, straightest tree had *some* curve to it. In the city, you had to search for a curve, though you could of course find them.

As for the smells, they were infinitely varied. Some were pleasing, others not. Most simply hung in the air. Ragweed suspected it would take a lifetime to sort through them all.

It was also hard to determine where city noises came from. They were nothing like the quiet rustling of the country. More like the music of the Be-Flat Tires.

As Ragweed continued to wander he heard a sound that seemed familiar. It took him a moment to recognize the train whistle. It came to him like the call of an old friend. In his meandering he had drawn close to the railroad.

He reached the end of the block. The railroad tracks were just across the way. Clutch's car stood on the far corner. He could even see her entryway.

Ragweed faced his choices: to board the train out of Amperville or to wait for his new friend to return.

He thought again about the death of so many mice

and the destruction of the Cheese Squeeze Club. With a sigh he had to admit there was every reason for the mice to be discouraged. Struggling against F.E.A.R. just didn't seem worth it. "I mean, like, maybe that's what city life is about," he told himself. But if he left, didn't he owe it to Clutch to at least explain why he was leaving?

"Stop making excuses," he told himself. "Go while you still have the chance. Face it, dude, city life isn't for you."

As Ragweed moved closer to the tracks, he noted the pile of junk where he had hidden from Silversides upon his arrival. Though he knew it was not the sweetest-smelling of places, he decided he could hide there safely, at least until a train came by.

A quick dart took him deep within the pile. "Phew!" he murmured. "Totally stinky." Detouring around some old cans, he found a high, dry perch that provided an unobstructed view of the train tracks.

"Which direction should I go?" Ragweed mused. After some reflection he decided he would leave that decision to fate. He would hop the first train that came from either direction.

"Except, no way I'm going back home to the Brook," he promised himself. "Not yet. Wouldn't be cool."

So resolved, Ragweed squatted down, fixed his gaze upon the tracks, and prepared to wait for as long as it took for the train to show up.

He had been there for some time when his eyes began to wander. Only then did he see that not far from where he was, near the heap of dirty-white clay chunks, Silversides was crouching. "Oh, bummer," Ragweed groaned. "It's her again. What's she doing *here?*"

Moving carefully so the cat would not notice him,

Ragweed edged himself higher on the pile in order to get a better view.

It was then that he saw what held Silversides's rapt attention. On the mound of white clay, some eight feet from where the cat crouched, a mouse was perched. To Ragweed's amazement the mouse was entirely white.

Ragweed had never heard of, much less seen, a completely white mouse before. His first thought was that he was seeing a ghost. He stared at this mouse intently to reassure himself that the mouse was in fact real. Moreover, not only was it real, it was very frightened.

Ragweed's speculations were interrupted by the sound of a whistle. A train was coming.

"Bummer! All I want to do is get out of here," Ragweed reminded himself. "Nothing but weird cats chasing weird mice. Too much. No way do I mess with this dude Silversides again."

Even so, Ragweed could not take his eyes from the scene. The cat was creeping closer and closer to the white mouse. For his part, the white mouse kept poking his head up, then ducking down into a hiding place. It dawned on Ragweed that the mouse was not aware of Silversides.

"Hey, dude," Ragweed murmured under his breath, "unless you do something fast you are, like, going to be a ghost for sure."

14
Ragweed Makes Up
His Mind

As the train whistle grew louder, Silversides continued to creep forward, drawing ever nearer to the white mouse.

Horrified by what was unfolding before his eyes, but not knowing what to do, Ragweed rose up on his hind legs. Silversides was too intent on the other mouse to notice him.

The huge train—headlamp flashing, bells ringing, motors roaring—swept into view. Every few seconds the whistle blew its lonely tune of mournful wandering. Ragweed could see nothing but boxcars, many of which had their doors open.

The train moved slower and slower until, just as it had done when Ragweed was aboard, it lurched to a banging stop. Boarding would be easy.

A deep longing came over Ragweed. He wanted to be home. He had been a fool to leave. Instead of hiding in the midst of garbage, he could be frolicking in the clear, bright Brook with his brothers and sisters. What was Amperville to him? Nothing but dirt, danger, endless talk, and F.E.A.R.

He glanced toward the mound of clay. The white mouse was still oblivious to what was about to happen to him.

"Hey, dude," Ragweed said, talking to himself, "like, that's his lookout. I mean, I'm out of here." Though he said the words, he remained where he was and kept his eyes on the scene before him.

Forcing himself to turn from what surely was going to be a scene of carnage, Ragweed darted toward the train. Halfway there he halted and looked back.

Silversides was crouched low. Her rump was wiggling. Her rear legs were tensed. She was preparing to pounce.

Ragweed's stomach churned. His pulse quickened. It was all too ghastly. Once more he began to move toward the train before stopping again. Could he just go and leave this strange white mouse to its terrible fate? "No," he said aloud, "I can't do it. It's too awful. Like, if I don't try to do something for that mouse I'll never be able to live with myself."

Glancing around, he saw that he had reached a spot that might enable him to distract the cat, yet still get to the train.

Rising up tall, Ragweed cupped his paws around his mouth and shouted, "Hey, dudes! Like, what's up?"

Startled, Blinker looked around. Then and only then did he see Silversides. Taken by surprise, he was terrified.

Silversides was equally startled by Ragweed. Her head snapped up and she looked about to see who had called.

"I'm right here, dude," Ragweed taunted, stealing a nervous glance over his shoulder to make sure his path to the train remained clear. "Remember me? The one who got away from you when I first came to town. The one who, like, popped Clutch's deck into your mouth. Remember? Yah, yah, you can't catch me!" he jeered.

Silversides suddenly seemed to understand who was calling her. Abandoning her pursuit of the white mouse, she started to move toward Ragweed.

"Hey, whitey," Ragweed shouted to the mouse. "Now's your chance! Run for it!"

Blinker, however, was too frightened to do anything other than blink and gape.

Not so Silversides. She leaped toward Ragweed.

Ragweed was ready. The instant he saw the cat coming, he spun around and dashed for the train. Even as he did, there was a sudden progression of loud bangs as mechanical couplings went taut. The train began to roll away.

Unnerved, Ragweed made a desperate leap in hopes he could grab hold of a dangling coupling hose. Not only did he fall short, but the train increased its speed so rapidly he was afraid to make a second attempt. He might be crushed by the steel wheels. He had missed the train.

Hearing a sound behind him, he whirled just in time to see Silversides barreling down at him, yellow eyes ablaze with wrath, sequined collar glittering, pink mouth and sharp white teeth fully exposed.

"Bummer!" Ragweed cried. "She's got me!"

Silversides took a giant leap through the air.

As the cat plunged down, Ragweed dove beneath her. His size and speed enabled him to slip under the cat, but so close did they come that Ragweed felt the cat's belly fur rub along his own back. No matter. By the time Silversides landed, Ragweed not only had passed her but was racing madly toward the white pile.

When Silversides landed, she was completely confused as to where the golden mouse had gone. She looked now this way, now that. She finally glanced behind her and caught sight of Ragweed racing away. With a yowl, she spun on the spot and tore after him.

Ragweed was aiming for the white mouse. Blinker, who had observed everything that had happened with little more than numb comprehension, saw Ragweed coming.

"Head for the junk pile, dude!" Ragweed screamed.

All that Blinker could manage was to open his eyes wide.

Ragweed reached him. Without ceremony, he grabbed one of Blinker's paws and yanked, spinning the petrified mouse around. "If you want to live, mouse," Ragweed yelled, "hit it!"

The mouse, shocked into motion, scrambled after Ragweed.

Coming right behind and gaining quickly was Silversides.

"Faster!" Ragweed cried. "Faster!" It took Ragweed seven running leaps to reach the pile. With no hesitation, he plunged into the stinking garbage, clawing desperately beneath the surface until he sank knee-deep into the trash. Turning, he saw he was safe, but the white mouse was struggling. Ragweed grabbed one of Blinker's paws and dragged him to his side.

From outside the pile, they heard Silversides yowling with frustration.

"We're safe," Ragweed replied. "For a while."

The white mouse was weak to the point of collapse. "Thank . . . you. You saved my life. I . . . had . . . no idea. Who . . . are you?" he asked.

"The name's Ragweed, dude. Like, what's yours?"

"Blinker."

"Cool."

Blinker looked around at the garbage. "Is . . . this your nest?" he asked.

"This dump? No way, dude. Actually, I don't even live in this town. Like, I'm just passing through. Where are you from?"

"I . . . I live in the nest where . . . Silversides lives."

Ragweed was taken aback. "Her nest?"

Blinker nodded mournfully.

"Are you friends?"

"Oh, no, not at all," Blinker assured Ragweed. "On the contrary."

"Were you, like, running away from her?"

"It's not that simple," Blinker said with a sigh.

Ragweed gazed at Blinker. This was one odd mouse. "Stay here, and chill," he said. "I'll go see what's happening with the cat. We don't want to be surprised. Then you can tell me your story."

"You won't leave me, will you?" Blinker cried.

"Hey, trust me."

Ragweed pushed his way up through the junk. He poked his head out of the top of the heap and surveyed the scene.

Silversides was sitting a few feet off, angry eyes fixed on the pile of garbage.

Ragweed returned to Blinker. "I think she's going to try and wait us out. So we need to chill out for a while. You cool?"

"I'm all right."

"Okay, go ahead," Ragweed said. "You were about to tell me your story."

"It's not very interesting."

Ragweed shrugged. "Just tell it like it is."

Blinker told his entire history, from the time the girl brought him home from the pet store to his escape.

"I thought you were trying to get on the train," Ragweed said when Blinker was done.

The white mouse shook his head sadly. "All I want to do is get back to my cage. I don't think I'll ever leave it again."

"Why?"

"The world is too big for me. It's wonderful but . . . very frightening. But what about you?" Blinker asked. "If you don't live in this town, why are you here?"

"Dude," Ragweed replied, "my life couldn't be more different from yours." He told Blinker how he came to be in Amperville.

"But the way you talk," Blinker said. "It's . . . different."

Ragweed, delighted Blinker had noticed, grinned. "That's the way city mice talk, dude," he said proudly.

Blinker sighed. "You and I have led such dissimilar lives," he said. "For example, you have a family. I have no memory of my parents or brothers or sisters. The girl in my nest told me I was bred in a mouse factory. Your nest by that Brook sounds so beautiful, so serene."

"It's okay, but way dullsville, if you know what I'm saying. Nothing ever happens there. Compared to all this, anyway."

"Oh," Blinker cried from the heart, "if I had a home like that, I believe I should never leave it. And yet," he added sadly, "though we have led such different lives, here we are, in the same predicament. Do you think we'll have to spend the rest of our lives here?"

"Hey, no way, dude," Ragweed assured him. "In fact, I'll go check on Silversides. Like, maybe she's gone."

Once more Ragweed worked his way up through the pile. When he reached the top, he carefully edged aside some moldy newspaper and spied out. Silversides was in the same spot she had been before. But she was no longer alone. Next to her was Graybar.

15

Trapped in the Garbage Pile

agweed slipped back to the middle of the pile where Blinker was waiting nervously. "Is she gone?" the white mouse asked.

"No way."

"What is she doing?"

"Waiting for us, dude. Worse, she has her friend, Graybar, with her."

"I never heard of a Graybar," Blinker whispered.

"Like, I don't think you want to, dude," Ragweed warned. "Ragged ears, scars, limps like a fighter. Know what I'm saying? Bad to the bone."

"I can imagine," a dejected Blinker replied.

Ragweed, unsure of what to do, looked around. On the one paw, garbage surrounded them. The stench was awful. On the other paw, it was full of edible food, which meant they could—if they had to—stay. But only for a while. At some point they'd have to get out.

Ragweed knew where he wanted to go—Clutch's car. It wasn't far. If they managed to get there, they would be safe. The question was, how could they get from the garbage pile to the Ford without being caught? One cat was bad enough. Two made escape almost impossible.

Ragweed wished Clutch were with them. He was sure she had a lot more experience in these things than he did. It made him think about how much he admired her.

"I am terribly sorry to have put you into such a predicament," Blinker offered. "And here you were about to go away."

"Maybe," Ragweed said, "but it was my choice to help you, dude, so we don't have to talk about that anymore, okay? There's always the chance we could outrun them. Like, how fast can you go?" he asked.

"I'm not sure," Blinker said.

Ragweed pondered. Then he said, "Chill. I'm going to take another look out."

Once more Ragweed climbed to the top of the garbage pile. This time when he came up it was by a large, mostly empty plastic bottle—curiously labeled "Dr. Pepper"—balanced precariously near the top. Careful not to nudge it lest he dislodge it and send it clattering down the pile, Ragweed surveyed the scene.

Silversides was where she'd been before, her eyes glued to the garbage pile. But she was alone again.

Ragweed was not ready to celebrate. Instead, he turned and confirmed his own worst fears. Not only was Graybar on the other side, he was sitting between the garbage pile and Clutch's Ford. What's more, he was waiting just as patiently as Silversides.

Ragweed returned to Blinker. "Silversides is still there," he informed the white mouse. "And so is her friend Graybar. We're surrounded."

"Oh, my," Blinker sighed, wiping away a tear. "It was an

awful mistake to leave the safety of my room. I should have been satisfied with what I had. What have I achieved?"

"Listen, dude, you did the best you could. Know what I'm saying? Check it out. You can either sit here and moan or figure out how to get to the next step."

"I suppose you're right," Blinker said, cringing. "It's just that I don't know what to *do*. I'm all bottled up."

Ragweed sat up. "Hey! Maybe that's the way to get out of this mess. It's like, risky. But hey, dude, I don't know what else to do."

"I'll . . . do . . . whatever you think is best," Blinker stammered.

"Okay, then," Ragweed said. "Keep behind me. And, like, no talking."

Followed by Blinker, Ragweed worked his way to the top of the junk pile, coming up by the plastic bottle's open neck.

"Now stay way cool," Ragweed whispered. "First, you've got to squeeze into the bottle. But don't make any extra movement. Once you're in, stay on the uphill side. That'll keep the bottle from tipping over till we're ready. You get it?"

"I . . . I think so. What about you?"

"I'll follow you in. Okay," Ragweed urged. "Go for it."

Whiskers trembling, Blinker poked his head into the bottle's neck, then slipped the rest of the way in. His slimness served him well. Within moments he was wading in brown liquid. The bottle teetered, but Blinker kept to the uphill side of the junk heap and the bottle stayed put.

It was Ragweed's turn. Bracing himself, making sure not to move too quickly, he squeezed into the bottle's neck, inserting his front paws first so as to take up less room and at the same time pull himself forward.

Ragweed was plumper than Blinker, so it was a tight squeeze. He had to push and kick. Even then he became momentarily stuck. It took all his strength to squeeze and pull through the last inch of the neck. His movement caused the bottle to teeter.

Blinker, not daring to move, watched anxiously.

Finally together inside the bottle, the two mice scrambled to find the right balance.

"Like, we did it," Ragweed whispered.

"I'm very glad," Blinker said, though he did not sound it. His eyes were very wide and his teeth were chattering. It was humid inside the bottle, and the air was heavy with a cloying, sweet smell. "I think we're in what's called soda."

"Wouldn't know," Ragweed said. He took a lick. "Killer sweet."

"What . . . what do we do now?" the white mouse asked. His voice echoed, as if he were calling into an empty well.

Ragweed tried to look through the sides of the bottle, but its curves distorted the view.

"Okay," he said. "Here's the way we'll do it. When I give the word, we're going to throw ourselves at the far side of the bottle, paws up, like this." He held his paws flat out.

"If we bop the bottle right, it should, like, roll off the pile. Won't matter if the cats see us. No way they can get at us. If the bottle goes the way I think it will, we'll be real close to my friend Clutch's car. Get inside that and we're safe, dude. Keep trusting me," he added when he saw Blinker's look of anxiety.

"I'm trying," the white mouse replied faintly.

"You ready?" Ragweed asked.

"Yes."

"Okay. Like, when I say go, dude, jump to the other side. We need to do it together."

"I understand," Blinker said.

"Here we go." Taking a deep breath, Ragweed began to count, "One . . . two . . . three! Like, jump!"

At the word the two mice leaped. With a lurch, the bottle began to roll down the side of the junk pile. Unable to stay on his feet, a suddenly helpless Ragweed tumbled head over heels. Blinker, who was used to the exercise wheel in his cage, ran with the bottle's spin. Even so, both mice received a complete soaking.

The bottle came down on the side where Graybar was waiting. Startled, he scampered away.

Inside the rolling bottle, Ragweed continued to turn somersaults, while a panicky Blinker kept running in place. When the bottle finally reached level ground, it continued to roll—thanks to Blinker's efforts—but now it began to spin, too. Unable to keep to his feet, the white mouse slipped. Blinker and Ragweed were hurled about at random, drenched in the sticky soda, until gradually the bottle came to a stop.

"Where are we?" a groggy Blinker asked.

After allowing his head to settle, Ragweed bent to peer through the neck of the bottle. "Cool!" he announced. "Like, I can see the hole in Clutch's car. We're pointing right at it. It's no more than a few feet away. And no cats in sight. Killer easy. Mouse, you did awesome."

"I did?" Blinker said.

"Staying on your feet and running. Gave us some extra energy. Tight. Where'd you learn that trick?"

"I run a wheel a lot."

"A wheel?"

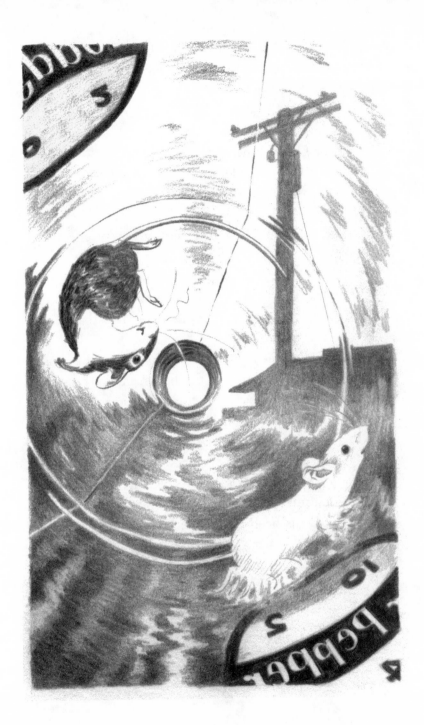

Blinker explained how the wheel in his cage worked.

"Weird. Anyway, the rest should be sweet. Let's get out of here. You first. Then I'll come."

"What if the cats see me?"

"If it gets too bad, like, forget me. Take care of yourself. Go for Clutch's nest."

"I wish I had never left my room," Blinker murmured.

"We've got to keep going, dude."

"I'll try," Blinker said dubiously.

"Hang in there," Ragweed said by way of encouragement.

"Okay," Blinker whispered. He squeezed through the bottle's neck. Once out he turned back and called softly, "Everything is all right. They're here, but they're still watching the garbage pile."

"Cool," Ragweed returned from inside the bottle. Shaking his rear legs free of the brown liquid, he slipped into the neck of the bottle and wiggled forward. The moment he did, he knew he'd made a bad mistake: He'd forgotten to stretch his front paws before him. Now they were pinned uselessly to his sides. Fortunately, his wet, slippery fur made his passage possible. By wiggling, twisting, and squirming, he managed to move forward until he finally poked his head out of the bottle top.

Blinker was waiting nervously. "Hurry," he whispered.

"I'm trying, dude, I'm trying," Ragweed replied, keeping his voice low. The next moment he stopped moving.

"What's the matter?" the white mouse whispered.

"Blinker," Ragweed said, panic edging into his voice for the first time, "I'm stuck. I can't move. You've got to help me. Pull me out."

Blinker started to reach for Ragweed's paws, which

were not there. "But . . . what shall I hold on to?" he cried. Jittery, he spoke loudly.

"My ears!" Ragweed cried. "Grab my ears!"

"But I'll hurt you," Blinker stammered.

Behind them, Silversides and Graybar meowed.

"The cats have seen us!" Ragweed yelled at Blinker. "Get me out of here! They'll bite my head off!"

"I'll hurt you," Blinker squealed.

"Don't worry about hurting me!" Ragweed screamed. "It's my life I'm worried about."

The cats were drawing closer.

Blinker grasped Ragweed's ears and began to pull. Heels dug in, he leaned back and pulled and pulled again. Slowly, painfully, Ragweed began to slip out. "More!" he shouted, though his ears hurt awfully.

With a sudden *pop* Ragweed burst out of the bottle. He came out so suddenly, Blinker tumbled backwards. As for Ragweed, he flew over Blinker, landing hard but not far from Clutch's door.

By this time the cats were sprinting toward them.

Ragweed leaped to his feet. "Run!" he shouted and hurled himself against Clutch's entryway. It would not budge. Though he banged and banged on the wood it remained stuck. Then he remembered what Clutch had told him, and he pounded the upper right section. The wood fell in. Ragweed followed. The second he landed, he jumped up and turned around.

With the two cats right behind him, Blinker was scrambling to get to the hole.

Ragweed dashed out, grabbed the white mouse by a paw, and dragged him inside, then flung the wood over the entryway—right in the cats' faces.

"Hey, dude, you do make an excellent entrance," said a voice behind them.

16
Some Ideas

"What's up?" Clutch asked lazily, not bothering to suppress a yawn. "I just got back, saw you weren't here, and went back to sleep."

"Silversides," Ragweed managed to say while gasping for breath. "And Graybar."

"Hey, what else is new?" Clutch replied casually. She gestured toward Blinker. "Who's the pale dude?"

"Oh, right," Ragweed said, rubbing his ears to take away the pain he still felt. "This is Blinker. Blinker, like, this is Clutch."

"I'm very pleased to meet you," Blinker murmured.

"Likewise," Clutch returned. "Hey, dude," she said to Blinker, "like, you've got killer fur."

"Thank you," Blinker said, blushing through his whiteness.

"Is it real?" Clutch asked.

"Real?"

"Or is it, you know, like, dyed?"

"I'm afraid it's the way I am," Blinker replied apologetically. "I . . . like the green fur on your head. And your earring."

"The head is dyed. The earring's totally plastic."

"They are very nice," Blinker said.

"Clutch," Ragweed said, "Blinker lives in Silversides's nest."

Clutch's eyes grew wide. "Yeah, right."

"I'm afraid so," Blinker admitted.

"What's the deal?"

"Tell her your story," Ragweed prompted.

Clutch listened with great interest, occasionally murmuring "Cool" or "Awesome." When Blinker was done, she turned to Ragweed. "How did you two dudes meet?"

"Just over by the railway tracks," Ragweed said. "Like, I was leaving town."

"Leaving town!" Clutch exclaimed. "How come?"

"Clutch," Ragweed said, "like, I've been here, what, two days, and how many times have I been chased by those cats?"

Clutch grinned.

"What's so funny?"

"The way you're talking, dude. Sweet. You got it down right. I mean, this golden guy is one fast learner," she said to Blinker.

Though pleased, Ragweed said only, "I mean it, Clutch. What's the point of staying? Like, sooner or later, I'm going to get totally wasted."

Clutch gave a thoughtful pull to her earring. "Hey, mouse, no one's saying anybody has to be a hero. But you don't want your tail leading the way, do you? I mean, lots of mice find city life too biggums. There *are* other places in the world. Except I bet you anything there's, like, danger everywhere. Being new here, you just notice it more. I mean, no one wants dudes telling them how to live, except you have to plant your head somewhere, right? Put it this way, dude: Being a mouse ain't easy *anywhere*. But hey, dude, if you want to nuzzle off, like, that's tight with me. Or whatever."

Ragweed, stung by Clutch's words, stared at her but said nothing.

Blinker, however, clapped his paws. "Why, that's . . . that's a wonderful philosophy!" he enthused. "Defend yourself or nuzzle off. I need to keep that in mind. You see, most of what I know is from books. But you—both of you—have truly *lived*. I'm so impressed. Thank you for saving me with your inspirational words."

Grinning, Clutch held out her paw. "Hit it, dude!" she cried.

Laughing, Blinker complied. Ragweed had not thought the white mouse capable of such emotion.

Clutch took Blinker off to one side, where they ate some crumbs. There she talked a great deal, telling stories about her life and the lives of her friends. Blinker listened with wide-eyed fascination, occasionally breaking in to say things like "Truly remarkable! Extraordinary! I am so impressed! It's a wonderful privilege to have met you." His praise made Clutch beam and talk even more.

In quite another mood, Ragweed kept to himself across the room. The more he reflected on Clutch's words, the more he had to admit she was right. Being a mouse meant you *did* always have to work extra hard to exist. It was the price of being small. That wasn't exactly what he'd had in mind when he had left his family to see the world, but it was true.

The young mouse sighed. The truth was, though he

had not done much so far, he'd gained a few things. There was his new friend Clutch. She was special. For sure, he would never have met such a mouse if he'd hung around the Brook, although it now made him uncomfortable that she was so taken with Blinker.

There were all the things he had seen, too, both from the train and in Amperville. Yes, he had experienced some amazing things.

And yet, what troubled him about Amperville was

that all the mice thought nothing could be done about F.E.A.R. Life might be dangerous everywhere, but country mouse or city mouse, that wasn't *his* style.

"If there were only some way . . ." he mused, staring up through the windows of the car at the sky.

Suddenly he heard Clutch say, "Hey, dude, what's up? You've got, like, a weird look on your face."

"Clutch," Ragweed announced, "I've made up my mind."

"Yeah? Cool. About what?"

"I'm going to crib here a while. But you know what I'm going to do?"

"What?"

"I'm going to deal with F.E.A.R."

Clutch started. "Take on F.E.A.R?" she cried. "Are you, like, totally out of your mind?"

"Maybe I am," Ragweed replied with a grin. "But, dude, a mouse has to do what a mouse has to do."

17
Silversides

"That was your golden mouse again, wasn't it?" Graybar asked a seething Silversides. The two cats were still sitting beside Clutch's old Ford.

"Yes," Silversides answered curtly. She was trembling with fury.

"And it's about the third time he's interfered with you, isn't it?" Graybar prodded.

"Yes."

"Hey, maybe you're getting too old for this," Graybar said.

"I'll never be too old to kill a mouse," Silversides snapped.

The cat continued to stare at Clutch's entryway in silence.

"I know whose place this is," Graybar said.

Silversides looked around.

"A mouse named Clutch. Sassy as they come. She skateboards. And she dyes her head different colors."

Silversides turned quickly. "Green?"

"I think so. I'll bet she's the one who got in your face at the club."

Silversides, who was sure of it, said nothing.

Graybar said, "Hey, speaking of colors, was that a *white* mouse I saw?"

Silversides grunted.

"Know anything about him?" Graybar asked.

"No," Silversides answered.

"Suit yourself," Graybar said.

Silversides started off. Graybar limped along by her side. "That golden mouse," he said with something of a sneer, "he's the one who keeps tugging your tail, isn't he?"

"Yes."

"Well, what are you going to do about it?"

"I don't know," Silversides admitted. "I'll think of something."

"We could have staked out Clutch's place," Graybar suggested. "Except there's bound to be more than one way out of that old car. Mice are tricky that way. You can't ever trust them to do what they should do."

Silversides grunted again.

"Hey, you want some dinner?" Graybar asked. "Got a couple of fish heads no more than three days old. A good meal will cheer you up."

"No, thank you," Silversides said. "I'm going home." Even as she spoke she remembered that the girl had said she could not return home until she brought Blinker back—dead or alive. Her teeth chattered with frustration.

"What's the matter now?" Graybar asked.

"Nothing," Silversides insisted. "I'll see you later," she said and stalked away.

Exasperated and angry, feeling that the whole world

was against her, Silversides roamed the city. Even so, she soon found herself standing in front of her own house. She supposed she could sneak in through her flap and the girl would never notice. She was probably in school anyway.

Eager to get back to her sheepskin and get some sleep, Silversides went to the back of the house and butted her head against her cat door. To her astonishment it opened only an inch, a space much too small for her to pass through. She banged at it again, but it refused to budge. Suddenly Silversides understood: The girl must have latched the door from inside. The small opening was meant to allow Blinker to get in, not Silversides.

Completely losing her temper, Silversides smashed her head on the door. All she gained was a headache.

Suddenly her rage faded. In its place appeared misery and grief. She saw it all: The three mice she hated most had banded together. She had been locked out of her home, kept from her bed of seven years, for something she had never done. Her own children, her grandchildren, had abandoned her. Did they ever think about her, ever come by for a visit? Ever get in touch with her? Never! No one loved or cared for her. She was alone! It was all the fault of mice! It was a conspiracy!

Sobs grew within her chest. Tears came to her eyes then rolled down her round, furry cheeks and fell to the earth. Miserable and forlorn, Silversides lifted her head and cried out a long, loud yowl of woe. "Nobody cares for me," she wailed. "*Nobody!*"

A window in the house flew open. The girl looked out. "Go away, you nasty cat!" she shouted. "Find Blinker!"

As Silversides gazed at the girl, the cat's mood shifted again. Her anger rekindled, she told herself she must put

aside all weak emotions. To do otherwise was cowardly. Mouse-like. If there was one thing worth living for, it was to revenge herself upon those three mice: the golden one, the white one, and the green-headed one. Once she found a way to deal with them, she would leave Amperville forever.

So resolved, Silversides tore the Amperville cat license from around her neck, dropped it at the back door of the girl's house, and marched away with her tail high.

18
Ragweed's Plan

The three mice—Ragweed, Clutch, and Blinker—were sitting around Clutch's nest, snacking on bread crumbs. Clutch was making a new skateboard from a Popsicle stick, shaping it with her teeth. Ragweed was doing most of the talking. A wide-eyed Blinker was listening intently.

"You see," Ragweed said, "like, what we need to do is show those cats that they can't go on terrorizing you guys. You have a right to live your own lives. Know what I'm saying?"

"Sure," Clutch said, spitting out a few wood bits.

"Okay," Ragweed continued. "So you have to stand up for yourselves. Like, from now on I'm making it a personal rule: No one is going to tell what me I can or can't do. No one. Ever. Like, period."

Blinker darted a look to Clutch to see what she thought before saying, "That's a . . . a fine idea," he said timidly. "But how could a mouse ever do such a thing? Aren't we—as Clutch said—too small?"

"Hey, dude," Ragweed returned boldly, "we may be little, but, like, there are lots of us."

Clutch grinned. "Listen to this dude," she said to Blinker. "Like, he's a talking ice cream." She laughed.

"Clutch," Ragweed pressed, "are you going to keep running, hiding, losing forever? Don't you want to be free to, like, play your own music?"

"You better believe it."

"Okay. Then I say it's time to do what you want to do."

Clutch laughed. "You're beginning to sound like my old mouse."

"No offense," Ragweed replied. "It's not that Windy is wrong. It's that he does nothing but talk and paint."

"Look here, Ragweed," Clutch said as she reached lazily for another crumb, popped it into her mouth, and chewed thoughtfully. "You aren't so off the mark, but just a while ago, duh, you were heading out of town on the first train. What's changed?"

Ragweed bristled. "I'd just like to show you what's possible, that's all."

"Yeah, right," Clutch said. "Show-and-tell time. But, hey, like, what are *you* going to do?"

Ragweed looked from Clutch to Blinker, then back at Clutch. Then he leaned forward. "It's called a new club."

Clutch put down her skateboard. "You serious, dude?"

"Check it out. A new club will be the best way to show those cats that you can't be put down. A new club will cheer you city dudes up. Give you courage. It'll be a place to chill out. To find your strength. Get all that working, and it'll be like, fighting back. But it has to be big—big enough to hold enough mice to fight back if attacked."

"Way cool," Clutch agreed. "Can the Be-Flat Tires play there?"

"That's the whole point."

"I mean, like, are you *really* serious?" Clutch demanded. "Not just sucking crumbs?"

"Clutch," Ragweed said earnestly, "in my whole life I've never been more serious. I mean, we'll get your father to paint some pictures on the wall. Your mother can read from her epic. Be-Flat Tires can play. Know what I'm saying? It'll be *your* club, dude."

Clutch gazed at Ragweed with laughing eyes. "Mouse, you got the lingo down perfecto sweet." Then she exclaimed, "But hey, mouse, killer idea! I love it. Put it there!" She held out a paw. Ragweed slapped it.

Blinker, though he wasn't sure what was happening, grinned.

"Now, what we need to do," Ragweed continued after the initial excitement had died down, "is find a place for the new club. That's where you come in," he said to Clutch.

"What do you mean?"

"Hey, like you said, I'm the new dude here. I wouldn't even know where to start looking."

"Oh, okay," Clutch agreed.

"Got to be different from the Cheese Squeeze Club," Ragweed went on. "A place cats can't get into easily or break down. But big. That's like, crucial. So there can be a lot of us. Know what I'm saying?"

"I hear you," Clutch said. She thought hard. "Hey, I know a place. It might work. In the humans' old downtown. You know, everything is deserted there. Including an abandoned bookstore. Used to have great-tasting books. But it has lots of space. Might work."

"Can we go check it out?" Ragweed asked.

"Sure thing, dude. But we'll bus out through the exhaust pipe just in case F.E.A.R. is still hanging around."

New skateboard in paw, Clutch led her friends out of her car nest through a long, narrow tube. Outside it was already dark. The moon was low. Only a few stars were out.

After a careful check to make sure the way was safe, Clutch dropped her board and pushed off.

"What is that?" Blinker cried, running along by Clutch's side.

"My wheels, dude. A skateboard."

"It looks very exciting," the white mouse said. "Do . . . do you think you could teach me to do that?"

"Nothing to it, dude," Clutch said.

"I would like that," Blinker murmured.

Though Ragweed said nothing, he wished he had thought of asking Clutch for lessons.

The three mice zigzagged across town. The streets and alleys had no sign of cats, humans, or even other mice. The only sound was the occasional crumpled aluminum can, caught in a wisp of wind, grating across the pavement like a broken rattle.

After some fifteen minutes of hard scampering and skateboarding, Clutch said, "Here we are."

They had entered a narrow alley. The only light came from a few flickering street lamps. A rusty garbage can overflowing with old, torn books dominated the way. On the back of the building was a window with a screen shielding cracked glass. A large, rusty padlock held a steel door shut.

"How do we get in?" Ragweed asked.

Clutch said, "There used to be a hole by this door."

After poking about the door frame, she called, "Sweet! It's still here." She propped her skateboard against the outside wall and dove into the hole. Blinker and Ragweed followed.

The three mice found themselves in a gloomy hallway littered with paper and heaps of broken-backed books. The floor was filthy. The walls were covered with tattered posters. Mounted low on the wall was a large wheel. Hanging beneath the wheel was a massive coil that to Ragweed's eyes looked like a snake. He froze.

"What's that?" he asked Clutch nervously.

"Not sure," she replied.

Blinker considered it. "I saw one of them in a book," he said. "It's called a hose, and it shoots water. Humans use it for putting out fires."

"Hey, this dude knows sweet stuff," Clutch said.

Blinker grinned shyly.

The mice moved forward and stood upon the threshold of a large room. On three walls were shelves, some of which contained a few books. More volumes were on the floor. Virtually all were broken. The whole area was littered with paper and broken boxes. The wooden floor was filthy.

Clutch gazed around. "Like, what a mess," she said.

"Yeah," Ragweed said, "but if we can clean it up, do you think it's usable?"

Clutch gazed about. "Never heard of a club this large. You could fit the whole town's mouse population in here. But, the main thing is, we'd have to work it so cats can't get in. Ever. Know what I'm saying? It's either the best or worst ever."

"There were screens on that back window," Ragweed

pointed out. "That entry hole was too small for them, and the back door is locked."

Clutch made her way to the front of the store and examined the main door. It was shut tight. "There's another hole up here," she called. "Too small for cats. Just right for mice."

The front wall of the store was mostly taken up by a large plate-glass window. Though it too was cracked, it had no holes.

On the glass were painted letters. Ragweed read them out loud.

THE LAST INDEPENDENT
BOOKSTORE

"What's that mean?" he asked, unable to make sense of it.

Blinker stared hard at the letters.

Clutch, more interested in the room, turned back to examine the space.

"Well, what do you think, dude?" Ragweed asked her.

"Be different," Clutch said, taking in the huge space with her eyes. "Needs an awesome amount of work. But it's cool. Just better be as tight as your tail is to your bod."

"Could we get other mice to help?" Ragweed asked.

"No problem," Clutch said. "I got zillions of pals. They'll help. Hey, what are we going to call this place?"

"Beats me," Ragweed said.

"I've figured out what those letters on the front window mean," Blinker announced. "We are looking at it backwards. It says, 'The Last Independent Bookstore.'"

"Decent," Ragweed said. "Maybe we should call this the Independent Club."

"Cool," Clutch said.

"In books," Blinker said shyly, "the sophisticated would call it Café Independent."

"I'm amped," Clutch exclaimed. "I mean, killer cool!"

"Then Café Independent it is," Ragweed said, seeing Clutch's enthusiasm. All three mice slapped their paws in agreement.

19
A Coming Together

Leaving Ragweed and Blinker to begin the cleanup, Clutch tore off on her skateboard to spread the news about the club. To each mouse she met her message was clear: "We're like, making a cool new club. Really sweet. Know what I'm saying? But we need some dudes to set it straight. Or whatever."

Lugnut and Dipstick were the first mice she informed. The two musicians reacted with great enthusiasm and promised to go to the abandoned bookstore immediately.

"Keep your eyes waxed for cats, dudes!" Clutch cried after them.

Clutch next informed her parents about the plan. Windshield, who was still working on the painting he'd intended for Ragweed, was particularly excited.

"Starting this new club," he enthused, "suggests that we mice have reached a new level of major turning points. It means mice are beginning to see themselves as a community. What has happened will affect many mice. These mice will affect still more mice. The movement will spread! The whole world of mice is about to change!"

"Way to go, Windy," Clutch said, trying to suppress a smile. "And hey, dude, Ragweed wants you to paint a mural on one of the walls."

"This is extraordinary!" Windshield cried, all but swooning with excitement. "This is *spectacular*! The ultimate turning point! Mice in the service of art. Art in the service of mice! It's . . . the *revolution*!" With that he rushed off to gather his painting supplies.

"And, Ma," Clutch said to Foglight, "Ragweed particularly mentioned you. Like, he was hoping you would do a reading of your work at our opening."

"From my . . . *Cheese of Grass*?"

"Hey, whatever."

"Clutch," Foglight said somberly, "you do understand it's a very serious work."

"Whatever."

"Do you think your friends can . . . appreciate it?"

" 'Course they can."

Foglight blushed with pleasure. "When will the opening take place?"

"If we can scrub the place up, like, in a few days."

"I would be . . . honored," Foglight said with great dignity. "But I do need to make some revisions." She hurried away to fetch her work.

Even as Clutch continued to spread the news, Silversides, having left the girl's house behind her, was moving toward Mouse Town. She had no particular plan of action in mind. Rather, she felt a random search might be productive. Maybe she would be lucky for once. The world owed her some good fortune.

For hours she slunk about Amperville, slipping silently

from street to street, sliding around corners and by for-saken buildings. A cloud-shrouded moon made the world seem more full of shadows than substance.

Padding along silently, Silversides paused occasionally to sniff the wind or to peer into a particularly dark place. Suddenly she caught a distinct whiff of fur, crumbs, cheese, and little paws. Mice! Their smell never failed to arouse her disgust and anger.

Trying to locate exactly where the odor was coming from, the cat moved to the left, then to the right, then to the left again. All the while she listened intently, ears swiveling, trying to pick up the slightest clue.

She padded silently forward. As the smell grew stronger, Silversides paused and scrutinized the area. The street she'd come to had once been a thriving business strip. Now it was abandoned. There was an empty grocery store. A stationery and toy shop. A restaurant. A book-store. A pharmacy. All were in varying stages of decay. Not one revealed the slightest sign of life. Some had their front glass broken or cracked. A few lacked doors.

Silversides inhaled deeply. The smell of mouse was so strong, she was certain it was coming from more than one mouse. She sniffed again. Yes, there were two, perhaps three mice. Perhaps she had uncovered a major mouse nest.

She examined the street in all directions but still saw nothing suspicious. Leaping upon a high windowsill, she achieved an excellent view of the entire street. There she crouched and waited.

Half an hour later her patience was rewarded. Along the far side of the street, against one of the deserted build-ings she detected movement. Something was creeping along close to the building. Silversides opened her eyes very wide and watched.

She saw two mice moving along by starts and stops.

Silversides was about to leap down and grab them when at the last moment she held herself back. Her instincts told her that there was more here than mere stink. She decided to watch the mice and see what happened.

The two mice came to a stop in front of one of the deserted stores. Its name was painted on the window in once-bright letters:

Silversides heard the two mice squeaking to each other, but all she could make out was the phrase, "She said to leave our instruments home for now." The next moment they popped into a hole and vanished from sight.

For a moment Silversides regretted not having acted. Perhaps these were the only mice involved. "No," she murmured, "have faith in yourself, cat. You smelled something more. Be patient."

When two more mice appeared, Silversides had the satisfaction of knowing that she had made the right decision. These two new ones were hurrying along the base of a dark wall. One, a rather fat mouse, was chattering with great excitement, so loudly Silversides caught some of the words: ". . . a whole new trend . . . a turning point . . . a revolution . . ."

The two mice paused before the bookstore door, then disappeared into the same hole the others had taken.

"My, my," Silversides murmured to herself. "Something *is* happening here, something big." She stretched her legs with anticipatory pleasure.

As she waited and watched, more and more mice appeared and made their way into the store. They came by ones, twos, and threes. Silversides watched them all with growing excitement.

Then for a long time, no more mice appeared.

Silversides was content. "If they go in, they'll come out," she told herself.

Folding her front paws beneath her chest, she settled in for the wait.

20

The Great Cleanup

It was two o'clock in the morning when Lugnut and Dipstick arrived at the bookstore.

"Hey, dude," Lugnut said to Ragweed, "we're here to be near!"

"Cool!" Ragweed said by way of welcome.

"Who's the pale one?" Dipstick whispered into Ragweed's ear.

"His name is Blinker. A friend of mine and . . . Clutch's." He made formal introductions.

Blinker held back shyly, preferring to look on.

Ragweed asked the two musicians to start clearing the main floor of bits and scraps. They set to with gusto, dragging and hauling.

Windshield and Foglight were the next to arrive. Right away Windshield took Ragweed aside and told him how important it was that this new club was being created. As he went on, Ragweed tried to be patient. "Mr. Windshield," he finally interrupted, "like, I have to work."

"Of course!" Windshield exclaimed. "Work lies at the

very heart of the mouse experience. It makes mice noble, even as it creates a common bond with all other mice."

"Like, what we need," Ragweed explained, "is some kind of mural on that wall. Know what I'm saying? Should be really sweet. Think you could do it?"

Windshield's eyes seemed to glow with fire. "What about something that expresses the total mouse experience from the dawn of existence to the present day?"

"Whatever," Ragweed agreed.

"Then I'm the mouse for you," Windshield pro-claimed. "What's more, you, sir, may be the first to know, I intend to make it my *masterpiece!*"

Over the next few hours almost a hundred mice ar-rived. Virtually all slipped in silently through the front door, found their way to Ragweed, and murmured, "Like, Clutch sent me, dude. I want to, you know, help."

Ragweed set them all to different tasks.

It was not long before the entire store was teeming with busy mice.

As for Windshield, he was staring at a blank wall, painting away—at least in his mind. Foglight was off alone in another corner looking grim—carefully revising her poem.

Blinker, meanwhile, found the courage to take on the task of dragging away pages of books that lay scattered about. Though he meant to work hard, he more often than not paused and glanced about at the activity swirling about him. It *was* exciting. These were remarkable mice. Ragweed was very brave and strong. As for Clutch, she was truly fascinating, quite the most fascinating mouse of all.

Yet Blinker reluctantly found himself wishing he were

back in his own room. "They don't mean to be rude, but they keep stealing glances at me," he kept telling himself. "It's because I'm different. An oddity. Not that there's anything I can do about it. I can't change my ways or my looks. I should be in my home, in my room, in my cage. I don't belong here." Still he stayed and tried to work.

The sheer dirtiness of the floor proved to be the most pressing problem. No matter how many mice scrubbed, it was clear it would take days to make the surface suitable for dancing.

Blinker approached Ragweed. "May I make a suggestion?"

"Sure, dude."

"That hose," the white mouse said timidly, "in the back hallway. The one used for putting out fires. Perhaps it could be used to wash the filth away."

"Way cool! But how?"

Blinker explained how the valve and hose worked.

Ragweed immediately saw great value in the idea. Quickly, every mouse in the store was recruited to help with the job. First, as many mice as could fit on the hose did so. With much lifting, pushing, and heaving, the hose—nozzle attached—was uncoiled, lowered to the floor, and dragged to the threshold of the main room. Then all the mice returned to the wheel and gripped it tightly.

"Heave!" Ragweed called. "Heave!"

As the mice tugged and pulled, the wheel began to turn. As it turned, a trickle of water began to flow from the nozzle, then a stream. The more the mice turned the wheel, the greater the strength of the gushing water.

"Hold it! Lower the pressure!" Ragweed cried. "It's too strong!"

The valve was adjusted.

When the proper force was set, the mice leaped down and gathered around the nozzle, grasped it in their paws and aimed it at the filthy floor. The power of the shooting water lifted the dirt and floated it away. By aiming the nozzle now this way, now that, the mice managed to flush the filth down the back steps of the store, into the building's basement.

The floor was soon clean. Hours if not days of work had been saved. The mice were so excited they didn't even bother to rewind the hose. Instead, they crowded around Ragweed and congratulated him on his idea.

For his part, Ragweed kept meaning to say it was Blinker's suggestion, but never quite did.

When Clutch returned to the store she was delighted to find that so many mice had responded to her summons. "Like, I'm stoked, dude," she informed Ragweed as they exchanged high fours.

"What should I be doing?" she asked.

"You, Lugnut, and Dipstick need to make a place to perform."

"Cool. What are you up to?"

Ragweed said, "I think I need to be, like, in charge of making sure those cats can't come busting in here like they did before."

"I hear you," Clutch agreed. "A 'Cats Keep Out' sign ain't going to do the trick."

"You got it."

Ragweed was about to go off and survey the store when he noticed Blinker off in a corner alone.

Still feeling guilty that he had not properly acknowledged the white mouse's contribution, Ragweed approached him. "What's up?" he asked.

"Nothing very much."

"The whole thing is pretty cool, don't you think?"

"Ragweed," Blinker said timidly, "I need your advice."

"About what?"

"I think . . . I should go."

"Go where?" Ragweed replied with surprise.

"To my human's nest."

Ragweed gazed at Blinker thoughtfully. "I thought, like, you were done with that, dude."

"I . . . I don't think I belong here. It makes me too anxious. I'm . . . different from everybody else."

"Hey," Ragweed said, "trust me. Everything new feels strange. Even being free probably takes some getting used to. Give it some time, dude."

"Perhaps," Blinker said. "Meeting mice like you and Clutch . . . Clutch is quite wonderful, isn't she?"

Ragweed found himself frowning. "Yes, she is."

Blinker considered Ragweed thoughtfully. "Ragweed," he asked, "are you particularly fond of her?"

"Yo," Ragweed said, wanting to change the subject, "that was great about the hose. Have any idea about ways to keep the cats out?"

"You mean, a security system?"

"That what you call it? Whatever. Like, we need to make this place really off-limits to cats. Last club they just blew apart. Can't let that happen again."

Blinker trembled at the thought of such destruction. "I'm sure you can work something out," he said. "But, Ragweed, I really, really do want to go home."

"Do you know the way?"

"No," Blinker admitted.

"Hey, dude," Ragweed urged, "you're going to have to loosen up a bit. Come with me."

"Ragweed," Blinker said in a whisper Ragweed had to strain to hear, "I . . . I don't want to stand between you and Clutch."

Ragweed nodded grimly. "Dude, if I know anything about Clutch, it's that she's got a mind of her own. We aren't going to decide anything. Know what I'm saying? She'll do what *she* wants."

"But—"

"Mouse, this club is going to open in a few days," Ragweed said, feeling some exasperation with Blinker. "Like, I promise, as soon as we check things out you can go on home."

"I want to go now," Blinker begged.

"But you don't know the way."

"I'll find it," Blinker said.

"Then go," Ragweed snapped and he went off.

Blinker watched him, murmuring, "He cares for Clutch, too. I'm only making trouble." Without saying goodbye, he slipped out of the store.

21
Silversides Learns Some Things

J ust before dawn, Silversides spied a white mouse emerging from the hole in the bookstore door. She could hardly believe her eyes. It was Blinker!

Unable to restrain herself, she flung herself down from her perch, streaked across the road, and trapped the mouse under her paws before he even realized what was happening.

Blinker began to cry. Silversides held him with one paw and cuffed him a few times across the ears with the other to make him stop squealing.

"It's about time we got together," she sneered, making sure her teeth were visible. "Now, quickly, what is going on?"

"Going . . . on?" Blinker stammered.

Silversides gave the mouse another cuff. "You heard me. There have been a lot of you vermin going into this old store. I want to know why."

"Please, I just want to go home," Blinker whimpered.

"You'll be lucky if you go anywhere," Silversides

snapped. "Talk fast or I'll bite your head off. Once more, what are all you mice doing in there?"

"It's . . . it's an old bookstore," the thoroughly frightened mouse said.

"Are you suggesting that you mice are going there to *read?*" Silversides hissed. "You're much too stupid. Hurry up! I want the truth!"

"You're hurting me," Blinker squealed.

"You won't feel anything unless you answer my questions," Silversides snarled.

"It's Ragweed . . . and Clutch," the mouse said haltingly. "He's setting up a new—"

"Ragweed?" Silversides interrupted. "Who's Ragweed?"

"He's . . . he's a golden mouse. He arrived in Amperville only recently."

Silversides's eyes gleamed as brightly as her sequined collar. "So that's his name! Suits him! And I'll bet anything that this Clutch has green hair. Am I right?"

"Y-yes," Blinker replied, even more frightened by what Silversides already knew.

"Are they friends of yours?"

"I . . . think so."

"Of course they are. You're a gang. A conspiracy. Go on. What are you plotting?"

"We're . . . we're not plotting. It's . . . just a new club for the mice," Blinker managed to say.

"A new club!" Silversides cried. "How dare they! They should be staying home and taking care of their filthy children."

"Silversides," Blinker pleaded. "Please, I don't know anything about it."

The cat, her paws still holding Blinker down, said, "Look here, Blinker, you want to live, to go home. And I suppose you want those two particular friends of yours to live, don't you?"

"Oh, yes, please," Blinker pleaded, "you mustn't hurt them. They're so kind. So nice—"

Silversides gave Blinker another swat. "Don't worry. I'll protect your friends. But first you're going to get back to this club and find out how I can get inside."

"Oh, no," the mouse cried in horror, "don't make me do—"

Silversides struck Blinker anew. "You either act as I say or your two friends will become cat food, do you understand me?"

"Oh, yes, but I—"

"Yes or no?"

"Yes."

With her teeth Silversides plucked up the mouse by the scruff of his neck and carried him, dangling, back to the girl's house, where she dropped him by the still-locked door. "The girl left it open for you, mouse. Not me. Now get inside and make sure she sees you. Do you understand? But I expect you to make your first report about the club tomorrow night. Right here. In the yard. Do you *understand?*"

"Yes," Blinker murmured.

Silversides leaned against the cat door. It opened just wide enough for a trembling Blinker to crawl through.

He went up the stairs of the house and into the girl's room. Once there, he took a deep breath, feeling a great sense of comfort and security. He was home.

He had started for the girl's bed when he fully realized what he had just agreed to do for Silversides. Dread engulfed him. "But at least Clutch and Ragweed won't be hurt," he whispered to himself. "The cat promised."

Instead of getting on the bed, Blinker went to the window, where he looked out into the world. It was dawn. The tears that fell along his cheeks were almost as big as he.

Silversides, meanwhile, made her way to Graybar's sewer home. When she arrived, the vice president of F.E.A.R. was deeply immersed in a meal consisting of the remnants of a double cheeseburger—with soggy pickles— along with a packet of french fries so limp they might have been spaghetti. Ketchup was smeared over a large portion of his face.

"What's up?" he asked when Silversides appeared. "Come for a decent meal?"

"I've got something going," Silversides announced grimly, ignoring Graybar's words. "Something big."

Graybar's eyes narrowed. "What?"

"We can wipe out a lot of mice in one blow."

"Whatever you say," Graybar replied with his usual indifference. "Sure you don't want some eats?"

"No. And Graybar," Silversides said.

"What's that?"

"I'm the head of F.E.A.R."

"What am I supposed to do, salute?" Graybar said with a shrug.

Silversides returned to the girl's house, found a make-shift place to sleep among the bushes in the backyard, and nodded off. But before she slept she reviewed her goals:

Get rid of the three mice.
End F.E.A.R.
Leave Amperville.
Never come back.

22

Blinker Makes a Report

O nce the girl saw that Blinker had returned alive, she sought out Silversides in the back-yard and told her she could return home. But when the girl failed to apologize for her false accusation, a proud Silversides refused. She preferred to remain outside.

With the cat out of the house, Blinker was free to roam at will. For most of the next day, however, he remained buried deep beneath the wood chips in his cage, where he slept fitfully or lay moaning in despair. Quite often he wept. Over and over again he wished he had never left the cage, the room, the house. How he wished he had never met Ragweed. Even more did he wish that he had never met Clutch.

"Oh," Blinker sighed, "I've fallen in love with the most amazing mouse in the whole world, only to be so weak that I've put her life in danger. The only way of saving her is by sacrificing the rest of the mice. But if Clutch learns about that, she'll hate me forever, anyway."

On the night after his return, Blinker, as he'd been told to do, crept out of the house and met Silversides.

"What I need," the cat said, "is complete information about what kind of security they're setting up."

"I . . . don't know how to get there," Blinker whispered in anguish.

"I'll escort you," Silversides assured him.

After leading Blinker back to the street where the new club was, she said, "Do you want me to come and get you in a couple of hours?"

"I think I can find my way back now," Blinker murmured.

"Remember," Silversides went on, "if you don't bring me the information I want, you'll never see those two friends of yours alive again."

Blinker, who had been considering running away, bowed his head in submission, convinced Silversides would do exactly as she threatened.

"Do they have a name for this place?" Silversides asked.

"Café . . . Independent."

"Café Good Riddance," the cat sneered. "Now go."

Blinker made his way into the old bookstore. The place was very busy. Windshield was attacking one wall with paint. Foglight was still in a corner immersed in writing. Clutch, Lugnut, and Dipstick were hard at work pushing and pulling a volume of an old encyclopedia across the floor with the intent of using it as a performance platform. Other mice were polishing the floor with bits of tissue. Still others were collecting and carrying out the endless trash, dumping it in the back hallway.

Blinker kept telling himself that he must let Clutch know what Silversides was planning.

"Hey, dude, what's happening?"

Blinker, startled out of his sad reverie, looked up. It was Ragweed.

"I . . . I . . . Oh, never mind," Blinker murmured mournfully.

"Where you been, dude?" Ragweed asked. "I thought you were gone for good."

Eyes to the floor, Blinker silently shook his head.

"Cool. If we're ever going to open this place, we need

every paw we've got. How about you and me taking a walk around the place and checking out security? Come on, dude, I can use your smarts." There was a hint of impatience in Ragweed's voice that made Blinker cringe.

"Oh, no, I couldn't. I . . ."

"Let's hit it, dude. Like, life is moving on!"

Sick to his stomach, Blinker followed along after Ragweed. The mice first checked the back door. The way had been blocked, making it impassable for any creature. From there they went on to check the front door hole.

"We'll post guards both places," Ragweed explained. "At all times. I don't think cats can get in, but dude, this place has to be, like, triple safe."

The reluctant Blinker in tow, Ragweed climbed the rickety old staircase to the second story of the building. At the top they found a room cluttered with junk from years past.

"Windows front and back," Ragweed observed. "But closed tight. Cool. Still, I think we better post sentries up here, too. They can look out on the front street and back alley."

"There's a hole in the wall over there," Blinker pointed out timorously. It was the size of a grapefruit and rather jagged around the edges.

"Hey, awesome, mouse!" Ragweed cried and hurried over to examine the hole. "Fantastic. It goes into the next building, dude. Way good."

"Why is that so good?" Blinker asked.

"We needed one decent bolt hole, dude. This'll be, like, a great one. I mean, if we ever need to empty the place out fast, we can zap up the steps and cruise out this way."

"I see," Blinker said. Knowing that he would be telling Silversides everything he learned made him feel ghastly.

Ragweed looked about. "I suppose we should check the basement."

"Ragweed, do . . . do you really think the cats . . . will try to get in?" Blinker asked.

Ragweed shrugged. "Maybe, maybe not. But, like, we can't take any chances. Know what I'm saying?"

"Maybe . . ." Blinker stammered, "it's all a mistake."

"What's a mistake?"

"Having this club."

"Don't be a dork, dude," Ragweed snapped.

Blinker was afraid to say any more.

The two mice went down the steep flight of steps that led into the basement. The area was small, dark, and damp. The dirt floor was spotted with stagnant pools of water from the hosing the floor had received the day before. A rusty furnace stood in one corner. Coils of wire and rope hung from the walls. Some broken chairs were piled one atop another. Bundles of old advertisements, along with a few boxes of decaying books, took up the rest of the space.

"What do you think that is?" Ragweed asked. He pointed to a large metal pipe that stuck into the room.

Blinker stared at it. "An old sewer hookup," he said.

"Mouse, how come you know so many things?"

"Well, I've not lived much. But I've read a great deal."

"Okay, what's a sewer?"

"It's a pipe that carries away dirt and waste."

"Where's it lead to?"

"Probably to a bigger sewer. But if it's unhooked," Blinker said, "and it looks that way because no water is coming out, I suppose it doesn't lead anywhere."

Ragweed hauled himself up, going from the newspapers to the chairs to a coil of rope until he reached the pipe. Clinging to its lip, he peered in. It was dark inside and had a bad odor. "You're right," he called down to Blinker, "it's not being used."

He dropped back down. "I don't see any way to get in, do you?" he said, looking around again.

"No."

"Then there's no point in posting a sentry here."

"I . . . I . . . think you should," Blinker stammered.

"You do? Why?"

Blinker hung his head. "Just in case," he mumbled.

"Yeah, I suppose, like, you're right. Let's go."

The two mice returned to the main floor. "Thanks for your help, dude," Ragweed said to Blinker. "And cheer up. Things are going to get better."

"Ragweed . . ." Blinker called as Ragweed started off.

"What's up, dude?"

Blinker's paws trembled. "I . . . I . . . have a . . . a confession to make."

"A what?"

"It's . . . It's . . ." Unable to find the words to speak, Blinker took a deep breath with the intention of trying again.

Before he could say anything, Clutch ran up and joined them. "Blinker!" she cried, "where you been, dude? I've been worried about you."

"You have?"

" 'Course I have."

"Why?"

Clutch grinned. "Hey, mouse, I like seeing you around."

Blinker bowed his head. "You do?"

"Right. So, like, where you been?"

"Home."

"I thought you were giving that life up."

"I . . . don't know . . . how," Blinker whispered.

Ragweed considered the two of them. They were certainly a striking couple, she tall and thin, gray-brown with the top of her head dyed green. He was small and shy, entirely white, with blinking pink eyes and a naked tail.

Sensing he should leave the two mice alone, Ragweed started to back away. Clutch grabbed hold of him. "Hey, dude, the guys and I have been thinking. Remember I told you about Muffler?"

"Wasn't that your lead singer?"

"You got it. The one Silversides took out."

At the mention of Silversides, Blinker paled.

"Anyway," Clutch continued to Ragweed, "with all your talents, dude, we figure you might be a singer, too."

"You mean, be a part of your band?" Ragweed exclaimed. He was rather pleased.

"Hey, dude, it would be awesome. How about giving it a try?"

"Well, sure, Clutch. Like, whatever. Just let me finish here with Blinker and . . ." He turned to where the white mouse had been. But Blinker was not to be seen.

23
Opening Night at Café Independent

The dim light of an outside street lamp slipped through the front window of the bookstore, providing a flickering pink light. The light cast letter-shaped shadows, so that the old name of the store was spelled out on the spotless, shining floor. All the old books that could be salvaged had been arranged neatly on shelves. Those that had pictures had been opened to provide decoration. Signs had been polished. One read "Children's Books," another "History." Some of the others read "Sports," "Animals," and "Health."

The mice had constructed a long counter out of discarded book boxes. Behind this construction stood Radiator, the fat mayor of Mouse Town. He was ready to dispense nectar, honey, and water from an array of bottle caps spread before him. Because of the grand opening, he was offering three kinds of cheese: green, orange, and white. Scattered throughout the room within easy reach were heaps of bread crumbs, sunflower seeds, and alfalfa sprouts.

The volume of the encyclopedia had been pushed into one corner in anticipation of the Be-Flat Tires's performance. Small tuna-fish cans were already in place for Lugnut. Dipstick's bass guitar was there. So was Clutch's new guitar.

Off to one side of the platform Foglight was still working on the finishing touches to her poem. On the other side of the room, near the art section, Windshield was whipping paint onto the wall with his tail. As he worked he kept mumbling under his breath, "Make the *turning point* a brighter yellow . . . Give the *trend* a more vibrant blue cast . . ."

Ragweed and Clutch stood in the center of the room. For the occasion she had redyed the top of her head bright red. Her purple earring, which was newly polished, dangled prettily. As for Ragweed, he looked no different than he ordinarily did, though he had licked down his fur to a neatness that would have made his mother proud. He and Clutch were standing before a group of five grim-faced, muscular young mice, all of whom had volunteered to be security guards.

"Okay, dudes," Clutch began. "You know what we're worried about. Do I have to, like, lay it all out?"

"Cats," the mice chanted in unison.

"And, like, you don't have to hear it from me, they are no joke. So you've got this awesome responsibility. Know what I'm saying? You all okay with that?"

The mice acknowledged their understanding by nods and squeaks.

"Cool. Now Ragweed here will give you your particular assignments."

"Brakepad," Ragweed began, speaking to a particularly large young house mouse, "you'll be at the front window, like, checking out the street in front of the store. That's an awesome stretch out there, dude. Killer activity."

"Hey, no problem," the burly mouse replied, squeezing his front paws so that his knuckles crunched audibly.

"Sparkplug," Ragweed continued to a young harvest mouse with large ears and bright eyes, "you take the back window. You're the one who has to check out the alley. Like, listen for weird sounds. Keep your eyes open for odd shadows. They can be something else. Know what I'm saying?"

"I'm hanging right there," Sparkplug replied.

"Piston, you and Seatbelt"—a deer mouse and a house mouse—"divvy up the back steps and the upstairs bolt hole. That's a really crucial place, so like Clutch says, are you guys are up for it?"

"We can handle it," Piston said for the two of them.

"Finally, Bumper, you've got the basement. You can stay on the top of the basement steps. Nothing but junk and an old sewer pipe down there. Even so, it has to be watched like the other places. You with me?"

"I hear you," Bumper, a short-tailed grasshopper mouse, replied.

"I miss anything?" Ragweed said, turning to Clutch.

Clutch shook her head. "Just keep your ears and eyes open to where it's at, dudes. Like, I know you'll be wanting to check out what's going here, where the party is. But—can't say it too many times—what you're doing is killer important. You let any cats in and you can nuzzle tomorrow goodbye. So if you get tired or need to check out, hey, no problem. Just come to me or Ragweed here. But those posts have to be covered at all times. Know what I'm saying? Everybody cool?"

The mice all said they understood and scooted off to their posts.

"Well, dude," Clutch said to Ragweed, "I think we're all set." She looked around the new club with satisfaction. Then she turned back to Ragweed. "Hey, have you seen Blinker?"

Ragweed replied, "I don't know. He hasn't been around today. I guess he'll show up."

"I worry about him," Clutch said.

"Hey, dude, you really like him a lot, don't you?" Ragweed blurted out.

Clutch eyed Ragweed. "Hey, he's way cool," was all she said before hurrying off.

Ragweed, wishing he understood exactly what Clutch was feeling, watched her go.

"First mice coming in!" Brakepad bellowed from his ledge post on the front window.

And indeed, the mice of Amperville had begun to stream into the club. They came alone, they came in pairs, they came in groups. However they came, they arrived in numbers. It was as if all the mice in Amperville felt the need to be at the café's opening night. The air was filled with great excitement.

Soon the old bookstore floor was covered with a milling mob of mice, generating a bubbling babble of squeak and squeal. Groups of mice were crowding together to talk. Individual mice strolled about and gawked as they inspected the new club or looked on as Windshield continued to paint his wall.

Clutch was very much the center of attention. Ragweed could see her red head bobbing about as she moved from group to group. She was accepting congratulations, even as she told anyone who cared to listen how the club came to be.

As the evening progressed, Ragweed remained in a corner, observing how things were going. From time to time he slipped away and went upstairs and down, checking with the security guards, making sure they were in place and attentive.

"The better job you do, dude," he told them one by one, "the better this place is going to be. Hey, face it. You guys are the most important mice in this place."

Some two hours after the first mouse had arrived Radiator worked his way to the platform. Once there, he sat up on his hind legs and looked over the crowd, rubbing his paws in satisfaction, nodding to first this mouse, then that, greeting most by name.

Finally he called, "Hey, guys, listen up!"

He was completely ignored.

The second time he fairly brayed, "Can I have your attention, dudes!"

That quieted the crowd. All eyes and ears turned toward the mayor. The only one who did not pay attention was Windshield, who continued to toil away on his painting as if no one else were there. "More purple where the mice are helping mice," he murmured.

"As mayor of Mouse Town," Radiator began, "it's my duty and pleasure to welcome you to the opening night of Café Independent!"

There was a raucous chorus of cheers, jeers, and squeaks.

"There are any number of mice we have to thank, but before we get into that I want to introduce Clutch's mother, Foglight. Foglight will read to us from the mouse epic she has been composing. Will you please join me in giving Foglight a Café Independent welcome!"

More applause and cheers as Foglight, looking somber, marched across the platform. When she reached the middle, she paused, looked sternly at the upturned faces and whiskers and began to recite her poem. She spoke slowly, enunciating each word with great care, using a free paw to provide emphasis. "From *Cheese of Grass*, Part Seventeen," she intoned.

"There once was a poetical young mouse
Who was considered a cantankerous souse.
Yet what the world never knew
Was that his fleas were more than a few,
And until this house mouse doused the louse, no one knew
he was really not a grouse.

Thank you."

For a brief moment there was nothing but stunned silence. Then the mice broke into wild applause. Foglight, smiling and bowing stiffly, backed off the platform.

Radiator returned to the stage. "Thank you, Foglight. Great poem. Thank you again. And now," he called out, "I want to introduce the mouse who had so much to do with this all, our own Clutch!"

Clutch leaped on the stage, wearing a grin as wide as her face, her red hair radiant, her earring bouncing.

"Hey, dudes," she called out, "this is, like, an awesome moment. Know what I'm saying? Check it out! But the dude who is really the force behind all this may be new to you. There he is over there, like, in the corner. My tight bud—Ragweed!"

All eyes turned to Ragweed, who, grinning, waved at the crowd.

"But all this talk is not, like, where it's at. I want to call the members of the Be-Flat Tires up here, along with Ragweed. We're going to swing into a little Café Independent music. You dudes ready for that?"

"Yes!" the crowd roared back.

Lugnut and Dipstick edged onto the stage and got ready to play. Lugnut set himself behind his guitar. Dipstick was primed to hit the drums. Within moments, Ragweed joined them up front and center.

Clutch turned to her band and snapped her fingers. "One . . . two . . . three . . ."

Dipstick stroked out the rhythm with a wild flourish. Then the other band members joined in with a rocking, rollicking beat of joy. Clutch nodded and whisked her tail. Lugnut leaped up and down. At first Ragweed hung back, head bowed, absorbing the beat. Then he stepped forward. In his low, husky voice, he began to sing:

"This old world is swinging on
As it keeps on spinning roun' and roun'
The sun comes up and the moon goes down,
But the dancing goes on and on.
Hey, mouse, whatcha doing tonight?
Hey, mouse, whatcha doing tonight?
Come on down and be . . . Independent!
Come on down and be . . . Independent!"

There was a general squeak of approval. The next moment the floor was crowded with dancers. They leaped and jumped and wiggled, and over and over again they joined in the chorus:

"Come on down and be . . . Independent!
Come on down and be . . . Independent!"

Clutch looked at Ragweed. Ragweed looked at Clutch.
They grinned at each other.

"Is Blinker here yet?" Clutch mouthed.

"Nope," Ragweed replied, and continued to sing his
heart out.

24
The Sewer

Silversides and Graybar moved silently through the streets of Amperville. Only when they came to the niche by the old sewer where Graybar made his living quarters did they stop. Fish bones, chicken bones, and assorted fast-food wrappers were scattered about. A half-eaten pizza slice lay curled up in one corner. Not far off was a bit of hot dog.

"Okay," Silversides said, "let's go over what Blinker told me."

"Sure thing," Graybar said, his tail twitching with impatience.

"Tonight at about ten-thirty—it's eleven now—the opening of this Café Independent club took place. The whole of Mouse Town should be there."

Graybar grinned.

"There's a dance," Silversides continued. "The mouse mayor gives a speech. The Be-Flat Tires perform."

"The *what?*" Graybar asked.

"It's a band. Clutch's band. And Ragweed is going to sing, too."

"That stuff doesn't matter," Graybar said. "Go over their security."

"There will be guards at both doors, front and back," Silversides said. "There will also be lookouts posted at the upstairs windows."

"Any bolt holes?" Graybar asked.

"You go up some back steps to the second floor, then into the next building."

"That's dumb," Graybar said with a smile.

"In the basement," Silversides went on, "is an old sewer connection. That's what interests us. There will be only one guard there."

Graybar nodded. "You got all this from that white mouse, right?"

"Correct."

"And you believe him?" Graybar asked.

"Yes."

"He wouldn't cross us, would he?"

"Blinker? Not a chance. I've just about scared him to death. Besides, he thinks I'm going to spare his friends."

"Yeah, right," Graybar said. He gazed at the rotting food. "Want anything to eat before we go?" he asked. "It's going to be a long night."

"We'll be eating when we get there," Silversides reminded him.

Graybar laughed. "Silversides, I like your style."

"Let's just go," the white cat said sourly.

"Sure thing," Graybar returned. "This way. Look out for slime."

The two cats headed into the sewer. Built of brick, the old sewer had a round, vaulted ceiling. In many places

the brick and lime mortar had crumbled and fallen into the old sluiceway. This sluiceway was clogged with refuse—moldy leaves, antique garbage, and motor oil, all blended together into a gummy, bad-smelling ooze. Such light as there was came only where grates opened to the street above.

On a level slightly higher than the sluiceway was a fairly uncluttered ledge. It was along this ledge that the two cats moved. Graybar limped along in the lead. Silversides, her white coat quickly streaked with muck, followed.

The cats walked in silence. Now and again, when something unusual turned up on the ledge—the limb of a doll, a grinning Pez head, a sneaker tongue—the cats paused, sniffed it, then moved on.

Silversides was excited but suppressed her feelings. She had the sense that she was approaching the culmination of a long journey. If Blinker had spoken true—and she had no doubt the terrified mouse had—she was about to trap most of the Amperville mice in one place. If she and Graybar did their task properly, methodically, and efficiently, they would be able to break the back of Amperville's rodent problem.

She reminded herself that she must make it her personal business to deal with this outsider, the one named Ragweed. She would seek him out first. Then she would deal with the green-headed one—Clutch. When all was done, she would return home and rid the world of Blinker.

After the carnage was over, she would seek out a comfortable rest home for cats and live out her golden years amid tranquility and calm. First among felines, she would accept accolades with dignified pride. Her life would be mellow and complete.

"Hold it!"

The cats had reached a place where sewer tunnels converged. It was a large, circular area with a ceiling higher and a basin deeper than normal. Other tunnels led off in different directions.

In the middle of the ceiling was a star-shaped grate, through which light came. "Let's see," Graybar said, "we're at Starr Square. It's where the city sewers come together. That pipe comes from Eudora Street. That one comes from Providence Place. Over there is Washington

Avenue. There's East Lane. What we want is Vail Way. Hang on, we're almost there."

The cats proceeded more slowly. Graybar set the pace. The sewer tunnel he took was smaller, narrower, older, and even dimmer than the one they had been in before. More bricks were dislodged. Now and again they had to squeeze forward.

"Lots of good stuff around here," Graybar murmured, "if you want to take the time to look."

Silversides shuddered. As they went along she became caught up in her thoughts again. How, she asked herself, had she ever come to such a pass, picking her way through such a horrid place with such a low-life cat, with the intent of wreaking havoc on disgusting mice? Could she have done something better with her life?

For a moment the white cat felt sorrowful. Was this all she had achieved, to be so full of anger and hate that she could think of nothing else but destroying mice? What would she do, she suddenly asked herself, when there were no mice left to hate?

"I think we've reached the right street," Graybar announced.

Silversides looked up and around. Here, along the curved walls, rusty pipes jutted into the main sewer at various intervals.

"One of these pipes should lead into that bookstore," Graybar said. "We just have to find the right one."

"Listen!" Silversides cried.

They lifted their heads. Faintly but distinctly came the sound of music with a heavy beat. With it came a thin chorus of squeaking.

"What's that?" Graybar asked.

"Mice," Silversides hissed. Just to be close rekindled her anger and rage. "It's their new club."

"It's going to be their *old* club soon," Graybar scoffed.

"Which pipe leads into the store?" Silversides wondered out loud. She listened intently. "The music is coming from this pipe," she said and hauled herself up into it, proceeding to wiggle forward. It proved to be the narrowest pipe she'd been in that evening. Still, it was clear of any obstruction and she was able to move forward with relative ease. As she proceeded the music grew louder.

The end of the pipe loomed before her. The music was quite loud. There was singing, too, plus a great deal of muffled tapping, which puzzled her at first. Then she grasped what it was. "Dancing!" she muttered under her breath. "How perfectly disgusting."

She inched forward. The smell of mouse was so offensive she was nauseated. But the strength of the odor was evidence of great numbers of mice.

Approaching the end of the pipe, Silversides slithered forward and took a quick peek out. The pipe led into a small, cluttered basement. Off to one side Silversides caught sight of some steps: easy entry to the floor above, where the mice were assembled. The question was, was someone guarding the stairs?

She took another peek. That time she caught sight of a mouse on the steps. He was sitting there, eyes closed, a dreamy look on his face, nodding his head to the beat of the music.

Withdrawing, Silversides backed out of the pipe.

"Any luck?" Graybar asked.

"We've got them," Silversides replied with barely contained glee. "There's just one mouse on guard, and he's asleep."

25

The Show at Café Independent

The Café Independent opening-night party was at full force. The Be-Flat Tires had completed their first set. Now, atop the platform, they were into their second. The whole room rocked with their sound. If anything, the band played better than during their first. Opening-night jitters were gone. They were playing together smoothly, listening to the grooves and beats, talking to one another, as it were, with their music. Sometimes Lugnut soloed, sometimes it was Dipstick, then it was Clutch. The music pulsed, the music soared, the music sang, the music *danced*.

The mice were enjoying themselves immensely. The floor was a rippling sea of bouncing, jumping, turning, wiggling, jiggling mice. Some had paws in the air. Others kept their eyes closed and moved as though in a trance. Tails waved low. Tails waved high. Some mice danced alone. Others danced in twos, threes, and even fours, paws touching, slapping, waving.

Not everyone was dancing. Some were on the side

talking, telling jokes, listening, watching. Crumbs were eaten, nectar and water drunk. A few even slept.

Windshield was still at work on his mural, muttering under his breath, sending splotches of paint hither and thither, to his own immense satisfaction as well as the interest and amusement of those who took the time to watch. Foglight had found a quiet corner, where she worked on yet another poem.

As for Ragweed, after his singing debut—which was very well received—he stood on the fringes of the crowd, watching. From time to time he made his way to the security guards.

"How's it going?" he asked.

"Way cool," he heard from now one, now another of the guards. "Like, no problems."

He examined the bolt hole upstairs and felt good about that.

He also checked the basement. Eyes closed, toes tapping, Bumper was sitting on the top step, dreamily listening to the music.

"Hey, dude, keep your eyes open," Ragweed warned with some severity.

"I will," returned the mouse. For a few moments after Ragweed had admonished him, Bumper did scrutinize the basement. All too quickly, however, he shifted his attention back to the music. Now and again he gave in to the temptation to close his eyes.

Ragweed, meanwhile, returned to the club upstairs, and for a while remained alone, off by a wall, watching the band perform. In particular he kept his eyes on Clutch. She was playing hard, head bobbing up and down, her face intense as her paws moved like summer lightning over the strings of her guitar, her lean, tall form vibrant with intensity.

Her fierceness fascinated Ragweed. At the same time he wasn't sure he knew her very well at all. What he did know, however, is that he would like to know her better. Was that possible? he wondered, wishing he knew how she felt about him and about Blinker.

Maybe, he mused, Amperville was not such a bad place after all. Maybe he should stay. Yeah, he liked the Amperville scene.

It took a moment for him to realize that Clutch was now looking right at him. She winked. He grinned back. Then she beckoned him toward her. Ragweed made his way through the teeming crowd to the band.

"What's up?" he called to her.

"Like, how about doing another number?" she shouted down to him.

"Sure," he replied, and hoisted himself up onto the book. He stepped forward, listening to the music, letting it seep into his head. He looked at Clutch. She looked back. He had no doubt then how fond of her he was. Recalling the song of the train whistle on his ride to Amperville, he began to sing, using the long, low, mournful whistle sound.

"Been traveling loooooong,
Been traveling faaaaaaar,
Beginning to wonder just where I are.
Have gone to the moooooon,
Have gone to the staaaaaar,
Wondering where I'm at on the calen-dar.
'Cause the world can be mean
Or the world can be nice

It all depends on where you've beeeeeeen.
All I know from all I've seeeeeeeen
Is I'll put my hopes on the rockinnnnnng,
rooooooooolling mice!"

It was at that moment that Blinker burst through the front entry of the Café Independent. Disheveled, dirty, and exhausted, it was all he could do to stagger forward, open his mouth, and cry out, "Clutch! Silversides is coming! Save yourself." Then he collapsed upon the floor.

The music stopped. The dancing ceased. Those nearest the prostrate Blinker backed away.

Clutch was the first to take action. She rushed over to the white mouse, knelt down, and gathered him up in her paws. "What, Blinker? What did you say?"

Blinker opened his eyes. "I've betrayed you. It's Silversides and Graybar. They're . . . coming to attack . . . through the sewer system. Make sure . . . you get away. I didn't know what to do. Please forgive me. I love you,

Clutch." With those words, the white mouse fainted away. Slowly Clutch lowered Blinker to the ground; then she stood up on her hind legs and looked around.

"The cats are coming to attack us through the sewer system," she said with a terrible calmness. "All you dudes be easy," she called out. "No panic. Like, we've got plenty of time to escape. Head up the stairs to the bolt hole. Youngsters first."

Then she bent down over Blinker again and nuzzled him.

The mice in the room fell utterly silent.

Ragweed stared at Clutch and Blinker. He did not know what to do. He felt like crying. He felt like screaming. But as he watched the milling mice begin to move upstairs, he felt a surge of desperate energy. What did he care now if he lived or died?

He jumped onto the platform. "No, wait!" he cried out to the mice. "You mustn't go! Like, are you going to run away all your lives? Check it out, dudes, are you going to give in to F.E.A.R. again? Are you always going to think life means being on the defensive? Know what I'm saying, dudes? There are a lot of us! We outnumber them. We can stop them! Like, this is our time! Those who are ready and willing to fight, stay behind and follow me!"

With that Ragweed leaped down and rushed for the back hallway. He did not look back to see if anyone was following. In truth, he did not care.

26

In the Basement

In the sewer pipe, just beyond the bookstore, Silversides and Graybar conferred in whispers.

"I'm sure we have them surprised," Silversides said. "That's the most important thing. They've posted only one guard. And he's asleep. I say we go fast, leap in and deal with him. It shouldn't be hard. Once we're in the basement, we can get up those steps easily. You head for their bolt hole on the top floor and block that. I'll block the front entrance. That way we'll trap them all."

"Sounds good to me," Graybar said.

"Remember," Silversides said. "Felines first. Now, follow me." With that she headed farther into the sewer pipe. Within moments she poked her head out of the pipe and into the basement. To her surprise, she saw no one. The post had been abandoned.

Silversides turned around. "That one guard is gone. Those stupid mice . . . Follow me." With that, the white cat pushed forward, reached the end of the pipe, and jumped into the basement.

The instant she landed, she crouched down and looked toward the steps again. No one was there. She went under the pipe and called up. "All clear. Get in fast!"

Graybar landed softly.

Side by side on the basement floor, the cats looked around and sniffed.

Suddenly Graybar said, "What happened to the music?"

"What music?" Silversides demanded.

"The mouse music."

Both cats lifted their heads and listened. There was nothing but silence.

Silversides felt a tremor of uneasiness. She pushed it aside. "Follow me," she said and padded quietly toward the steps. Graybar, looking around nervously, came a little way behind.

At the foot of the steps Silversides paused. "When we get to the top, plunge in, grab who you can, and put an end to their miserable lives. Just don't forget the two I want: the golden mouse and the one with green hair. Understood?"

"Sure, Silversides. I know all about that. Now let's get going."

"Felines first," Silversides muttered again and began climbing the steps.

She paused to listen and sniff again. Though the smell of mouse was almost overpowering, still she heard nothing.

She continued to move up until she reached the last riser. Once there she lifted her head and found herself staring directly into the bright brass nozzle of a water hose. Surrounding it, holding on to it, aiming it right at her, was a horde of mice. In the front of them stood Ragweed.

The moment Silversides lifted her head, Ragweed shouted, "Blast her!"

The hundred or so mice who were clinging to the valve wheel turned it. Instantly, water surged through the old canvas hose and shot out the nozzle. It was all the mice could do to hold on and keep it steady. But their aim was true. A blast of water as powerful as a cannon shot struck Silversides squarely in the face. It came with such surprise and force that it flung her head over heels back down the steps. As she tumbled she bowled into Graybar, knocking him down, too.

When the cats reached the bottom, they shook their heads and soggy bodies and tried to regroup. "At them!" Silversides howled, to rally her comrade.

Ragweed was ready at the top step. "Drag the hose forward," he ordered. The mice hauled the gushing hose with shouts of "Heave! Heave! Heave!"

The stream of water was now aimed down at the already stunned cats. Once again, they were struck hard.

Graybar attempted to climb the steps. He managed to gain two before the hose was aimed right at him. With a whoosh, he was washed to the very bottom again.

Now Silversides, soggy with water, eyes awash, tried a new attack. She met the same watery barrage as did Graybar, with the same results.

As the water continued to pour forth, the basement began to fill with water. The cats found themselves slipping, sliding, and floundering in the resulting mud. It was impossible to stand.

"Forward!" Ragweed commanded. The mice began to drag the hose down the steps, the nozzle aimed first at Silversides, then at Graybar.

Three times the cats attempted to climb the steps.

Three times they were hosed back by the powerful flow of water.

Graybar bolted. Up to his belly in cold water, he half scrambled, half swam to the open sewer pipe and crawled in. With wet fur plastered to his body, he was little more than skin and bones. He did not even look back to see if Silversides was coming with him.

Silversides tried yet another attack. With the hose still gushing, the water level in the basement rose quickly. The cat had nothing solid to stand on. The water began to drain into the sewer pipe. As it did, it flushed away everything in the room. That included Silversides.

The last the mice saw of Silversides was her bewildered face filled with rage and indignation as she flowed backward out of the basement and into the sewer pipe. She left nothing but her sequined collar, which soon followed her into the pipe.

For some moments afterward, the mice kept the hose aimed at the sewer pipe, wanting to be certain the cats did not return.

Finally it was a triumphant Ragweed who cried, "Hey, dudes, time to celebrate!"

27
A Goodbye

Three days later, Ragweed stood by the Amperville railway tracks, waiting for a train to arrive. With him were Clutch and Blinker. From off in the distance they heard the sound of the approaching train whistle.

"I mean," Clutch was saying to Ragweed, "like, there's no reason you have to go. Blinker and I would really like it if you hung around."

Ragweed smiled gamely. "Hey, dude, it's a big world out there. And I'm one small mouse. Like, there's a lot to see. Know what I'm saying? Anyway, one of these days I'll come back. Then I can visit with you guys. Teach your kids a trick or two."

"Check it out," Blinker said with a shy grin.

"Anyone see Silversides or Graybar yet?"

Clutch grinned. "Far as anyone can tell, they, like, left town. Someone said they took a train. All I know is they're gone. Totally sunk."

"Killer sweet," Ragweed agreed as the sound of the train whistle grew quite loud. "Only now it's my turn."

"Dude," Clutch said, becoming serious, "I just want to say you are one awesome mouse. I mean, like, you've done it all. You may be a country mouse, but you're way world class out of here. In fact, everyone connected with the club agreed we should change the name. From now on it's Club Ragweed."

"Awesome, dude," returned Ragweed, grinning broadly.

"But just to show you how Blinker and I feel," Clutch said, "we've got a present for you." She reached up and removed her purple plastic earring. She held it out so that the bead dangled from her paws. "We'd sort of like to give this to you, dude. I mean, if you want it, that is."

Ragweed took the earring gently. He was deeply moved.

"When you wear it, Ragweed, think of us and dance," Blinker suggested.

"Like, long as you wear it," Clutch added, "you'll never back down to any bully."

"I hear you," Ragweed said.

"Want me to put it on, dude?" Clutch asked.

"Be way cool."

Clutch fixed the earring to Ragweed's left ear. "Glad you came, dude." She gave the same ear a nuzzle as she added, "Dude, you totally buttered the muffin."

Blinker nuzzled his other ear.

The next moment all three mice embraced.

The train came slowly into view, headlight flashing, bells ringing, whistle sounding. Its arrival ended with a loud bang.

"Do you know where you're going?" Blinker asked.

"Hey," Ragweed said, "I've seen the city. Time to explore the forest."

With that he scampered up the coupling hose, moved along a boxcar gutter, and slipped inside.

Once settled, he looked out. Side by side, Blinker and Clutch were looking up at him.

The train lurched forward. Fighting tears, Ragweed waved goodbye with one paw, touching his new earring with the other.

"Hey, dude," Clutch cried, "don't forget!"

"Forget what?" Ragweed shouted back.

"A mouse has to do what a mouse has to do!" Clutch called. "Know what I'm saying?"

"Yo, baby," Ragweed shouted back, "like, I do!"

With a great shriek, the train gathered speed. Clutch and Blinker watched Ragweed go. Then, paw in paw, they headed for home.

Ragweed turned away at last and stared glumly at the passing world through the open door of the boxcar. Now and again he touched his new earring. But when the train whistle blew its mournful tune he found it impossible not to break into song:

"A mouse will a-roving go,
 Along wooded paths and pebbled ways
 To places high and places low,
 Where birds do sing 'neath sunny rays,
 For the world is full of mice, oh!
 For the world is full of mice, oh!"

Then Ragweed cupped his paws around his mouth and with all his strength shouted, "Dimwood Forest, here I come!"